QUEER
FOLK
TALES

Sikander and the Prince: Sikander was struck by the sheer beauty of this young man, swathed around with scarlet silks.

QUEER FOLK TALES

A BOOK OF LGBTQ+ STORIES

KEVIN WALKER

The
History
Press

To Mr Wolf

First published 2020

The History Press
97 St George's Place, Cheltenham,
Gloucestershire, GL50 3QB
www.thehistorypress.co.uk

British Library Cataloguing in Publication Data.
A catalogue record for this book is available from the British Library.

ISBN 978 0 7509 9380 7

Typesetting and origination by The History Press
Printed and bound in Great Britain by TJ International Ltd.

CONTENTS

INTRODUCTION

Welcome to my collection of stories all about queer folk. As a professional storyteller of many years' standing, I had noticed that there were few queer tellers who actually told queer stories. I began to slowly introduce some into my repertoire until one day another storyteller suggested that I should create a whole performance piece based on them. At first, I was hesitant. How would it be received? Who would be my audience? Then it took off and Faerie Looking to Meet Unicorn: A Reet Set of Queer Tales was born. I trialled it out at several storytelling clubs until I was happy with the format.

The audience reaction was amazingly positive, although there were some telling comments. One person said they would not have attended if they had realised what the content of the evening was going to be about, and another said that while listening to the stories they were always looking/waiting for the LGBT aspect, which was a slight distraction. I thanked them for their comments, pointed to the clear advertising and added that I totally agreed as I felt the same when I listened to conventional storytelling, it generally being heterosexual. Visibility was of paramount importance and my collection of stories grew.

There are few queer stories out there in traditional folk tale land, and I found myself reimagining or recreating known folk tales before finally writing my own stories. I had such fun. Stories I had heard being told by other tellers either relied on the dreadful humour of the eighties and nineties sitcoms, which sadly many modern audiences still found funny, or were *too* respectful and lacked any power. 'All the nicest guys I met at college turned out to be gay' is so condescending. We are *not* all nice because we are human and have imperfections just like anyone else. These stories were usually told by storytellers who were not from the LGBTQ+ community – cultural appropriation?

So, here you are, my attempt at a collection of queer-based tales that 'represent' friends from my community as best I can. I hope that you will laugh, cry and wince at the trials and tribulations of characters who just happen to be queer.

I am still collecting and writing new stories for my collection, so if you ever discover a story or an idea for a queer story that you think I might be interested in it, then please send it to me through my website, I would love to work on them. I have just written a ghost story and a follow-up story to the film *Some Like It Hot*, so my range is quite wide. Have fun reading. I had a ball writing this.

1

SIKANDER AND THE PRINCE

This is the first LGBTQ+ story that I ever wrote and performed, based on a story told to me by another storyteller. I loved the motif: 'Ask in the correct way and it might be granted to you.' I reworked the whole story to become punchier and queer friendly and now it is my favourite tale to tell. And the perfect way to open this collection.

Sikander stood looking up at the palace fortress that is the Alhambra and yelled, 'How is it that God can choose some to live in such absolute splendour and yet condemns others to live in the gutter?'

His grandmother, his *jaddati*, smiled at the tall, passionate young man and thought about how much he had changed over the years from that little scrap of a mewling baby, placed in her arms when his parents had been taken by the plague, to a confident man who knew exactly what he wanted from life.

'Well, you know what I always tell you,' she said. 'If you ask in the correct way, sometimes wishes can happen!'

He turned and looked at the woman who had been his mother, father and grandmother, providing for and nurturing him despite their poverty. He smiled and went over to hug her.

'It has always worked for me,' said his grandmother.

He took a step away from her, turned and, feeling a little foolish, closed his eyes and said, 'Please, if there is a way, even a small way, to make me part of palace life, please, make it happen.'

The next day Sikander was down in the plaza, the town square in Granada, where men gathered each morning hoping to be chosen for work. Suddenly, two richly dressed men trotted into the square on their fine Arab stallions and began pointing at various men. Sikander stood head and shoulders above the rest of the crowd and he was selected along with four other strapping young lads.

'Follow us,' the riders shouted, and they trotted out of the plaza and up the winding street. Sikander and the other men scuttled after them, trying their best to keep up with the horses. The road they followed wound upwards and soon, to Sikander's disbelief, they made their way along the parade that led to the fine gates of the Alhambra Palace and into the secret world of the sultan's compounds. He soon found that he had been chosen to be part of a group of workers who cared for many aspects of the palace buildings and grounds. At last, he was part of palace life!

In the heat of the day, the work was hard. There was lots of sweeping, carrying and running around but Sikander loved it.

The palace compounds were beautiful. The various palaces and apartments were built from the most intricate of materials, and everywhere there were carvings and tiled walls and floors. Exotic plants grew in the many gardens, but it was the water that amazed Sikander the most. Water, that most precious of commodities, flowed, trickled or glistened in huge pools everywhere. There were fountains with water spouting from the mouths of lions and other creatures, and narrow canals and rivulets carrying cool, clear water to large, still pools filled with fish. The air was cooled by the water, the senses calmed by its sounds and the reflections in the water mirrors were intoxicating. A piece of heaven had been created on the top of this high hill and Sikander was now a part of it. In a small way.

He worked so hard that he was instructed to come back the next day and in time he became a permanent fixture. Now, when he arrived in the morning, the guards on the gate waved to him and exchanged cheery comments. The work was so varied that Sikander loved the daily challenges and he became a valued employee. His pay was a great help at home too and his grandmother was able to take it easier.

Some time later, Sikander and a team of men were working near the main gate tidying the palm trees that grew over the road. He had climbed high to get to the crown of a palm in order to cut away the dying brown fronds. He sawed through them and they crashed to the ground so that the rest of the team could collect them and place them on a cart. It was hard, hot and dusty work but the team were in good spirits and the banter was loud. Sikander was hacking at a frond when he realised that the men below had gone quiet. He stopped what he was doing and looked down. They had dropped their tools and brushes and were standing by the side of the road, staring down the hill towards the city.

'It's him,' one of the men shouted. 'He's back, the prince is back!'

Sikander had a better view from high in the tree and sure enough he could see a distant procession coming towards them: soldiers on horseback, flags and banners, and the unmistakeable sound of trumpets and horns. As the procession came closer, Sikander could make out the colours and the emblems on the banners. The sounds were getting louder, the excitement growing and then, he saw him – the prince. Riding near the very front of the procession, on a magnificent black stallion, dressed in bright red silks, was the proud, upright figure of their beloved prince.

Sikander changed his grip on the tree to swing round and get a better view, but he very nearly let go in shock as he and the prince caught each other's eye. He was struck by the sheer beauty of this young man: olive skin, his black hair and beard and his large, dark eyes, all swathed around with scarlet silks. The prince smiled to see this young man hanging high from a tree and gracefully waved in his direction.

'Oh Grandmother, if only you could have seen him. He is magnificent. Oh, how I would love to come face to face with him.'

'Well, you know what I always say. Ask in the correct manner and it might just happen!'

Sikander smiled at his *jaddati* and closed his eyes. 'Please, if it is possible, please can I come close to my prince?'

The next day there was quite a commotion when Sikander arrived for work. The palace had water channels running everywhere around the grounds and through the buildings. Water for cooling, for pleasure, water to irrigate all the gardens and beautiful plants, and water for the cleaning and sluicing out the latrines. And of course, all that water must drain somewhere. Well, overnight, there had been a blockage at the lower main drains, and rank-smelling sewage had spilled everywhere. Sikander's team was sent in to clear the blockage and clean up the mess. All the men stripped to the waist and waded in, reaching deep into the slurry to clear the runoff point. It was filthy work but, as usual, the men were in high spirits and the air was filled with jovial banter.

Sikander was just reaching deep down into the grime when he realised that all had gone quiet around him. Standing up, he wiped his eyes so he could see more clearly, and when he looked to the main path, who should be standing there but the prince! He was wearing his usual scarlet robes but held the end of one of his scarves over his nose to mask the smell. His brow was furrowed but his face lit up in a glorious smile when he saw Sikander standing there, mouth open, covered in slurry but with two clean patches where he had wiped his eyes. The smile turned to a laugh, not an unkind one. He realised how necessary was this work that the men were carrying out, but he laughed, nonetheless. The other men laughed too and waved to the prince as he hurried away.

'Oh Grandmother, I know I wished to come close to my prince, but I didn't mean like that!'

His grandmother had to hold back a laugh as she threw buckets of water over her grandson to clean away the grime.

'Well, you know what I always say ...'

'No, Grandmother,' Sikander cut in. 'I have tried that way and look what happened? No, I will try my way.'

When he was clean and dry, he put on his best clothes and made his way to the palace grounds through the fading light of the late evening. He was well known by now, so no one challenged him. He came to the high wall that surrounded his prince's private dwelling, chose a tree that had overhanging branches and climbed up so that he could see into the grounds. The light was dimming, and lanterns had been lit. At last he saw the prince, his prince, dressed in scarlet silks, walk on to one of the patios and recline on a day bed. A servant came forward with a silver tray and offered him some food. The prince selected a ripe fig. Sikander watched transfixed as he gently felt and caressed the fig, held it close to his face and smelled it and then finally dug both his thumbs into the plump fruit, tearing it open to expose the glistening, moist flesh. Juice ran down the prince's hand and wrist and he relished licking the sweetness dry.

'Oh Grandmother, if I could have only been closer. To be there with him and able to offer my prince such a fruit and wipe his hand with a soft cloth.'

'Well, you know ...'

'No, Grandmother, I will do it my way.'

The next evening, Sikander made his way to the palace wall once again and climbed the tree. He sat and waited as the light dimmed and the lanterns were lit. Soon, his prince, again resplendent in scarlet satin, came walking down a garden path in the soft light. Sikander watched as he stopped now and again to take in the perfume of the flowers that grew everywhere. One by one, a rose or a spray of jasmine was pulled forward by a strong but gentle hand and held close to the prince's face, and Sikander could see by his smile and the glint in those beautiful, dark eyes, just how much pleasure he took in their fragrance and touch.

'Oh Grandmother, if the prince could only hold me that close to his face.'

'Well, as I keep saying, ask in the correct way and it might just happen.'

Sikander could not stop himself. His eyes immediately closed, and he whispered, 'Please, if it is possible, let me be close to the prince amongst his flowers.'

His mind wandered to the image of the dark features of his prince, encircled by the customary scarlet satin. And as his mind wandered, he slowly became aware that there was a gentle breeze blowing on his face and he felt as though he was gracefully swaying. He slowly opened his eyes and was surprised to find that he was no longer in his house with his grandmother but standing among flowers in a garden. With mounting excitement, he knew that this was the garden of the prince, and when he looked down, he realised he was no longer human but had transformed into a beautiful flower! When he looked up, here was his prince, walking along the path towards him, stopping now and again to take the blooms of a flower and hold them closely to his face. Sikander began to quiver with anticipation at the thought of his prince selecting him and holding him oh so close. As the prince came nearer, Sikander held up his blossomy head as high as he could so the prince would see him. And see him he did. He stopped for the shortest while, smiled but then walked on, leaving Sikander in full flower among the other plants.

You see, in Sikander's mind, he had conjured the image of the prince with dark, dark features surrounded by scarlet and had transitioned himself into a deep red poppy with a black centre. A beautiful flower yes, but a flower that not many would smell or pick. A plucked poppy soon loses its petals and it is thought that if you sniff a poppy it can result in headaches. So, although the prince admired his beauty, he walked on by.

Sikander's blossomy head drooped forward in sadness and one by one, his petals began to drop, leaving just that black centre. What could he do now? He stood in that garden day after day in the scorching Andalucian sun. His leaves dried and fell away, his stalk became brittle and hard, and his head began to dry and swell with sadness. And the long days and nights seemed endless.

But then, one morning, Sikander heard whistling and when he looked up, he saw another man skipping up the path. A rotund man dressed all in white and quite dusty! It was the palace baker.

'Now, where is that large poppy head I have been keeping my eye on for the last few weeks? Ah yes, here it is. Blue poppy seeds, the favourite flavouring of the prince.'

And with that, he carefully broke off Sikander's head and cupped him gently in the palm of his hand. He carried him into the kitchen and spilled Sikander's seed into a little bowl. He began to make bread dough and when it came to the final kneading, half of the seeds were sprinkled into the dough and folded in. The dough was divided up into balls, brushed with egg and then coated with the remaining seeds. The dough balls were covered and left in the sun and Sikander began to swell with pride at the thought of at last being with his prince. A short time followed in the oven and when the bread cakes were removed, the baker clapped his hands.

'Oh, the prince will so enjoy these.'

Sikander was arranged on a silver platter and a servant carried him out into the soft light of a lantern-lit evening and presented him to the prince on his day bed.

'My goodness, these smell wonderful,' gasped the prince.

He sat upright and hovered his hand above the platter, deciding which cake to choose. Sikander felt almost sick with excitement. The prince selected one and held it close to his face to smell that fresh-baked aroma. He gently squeezed the plumpness of the crusty little fellow and then roughly dug both his thumbs into the warm fleshy texture of the freshly baked bread. Sikander thought he would die of pleasure as the prince inhaled the smell of bread and then, taking one half, bit into the mixture of crustiness and softness and devoured it with obvious pleasure.

So Sikander was united with his prince at last.

Now the prince really did relish the taste and texture of blue poppy seeds, but his belly did not. It was unfortunately one of those foodstuffs that the prince really should not eat too much of and that night, he finished the whole batch.

Yes, Sikander had at last been with his prince but alas, it would prove to be only a passing relationship.

2

THE BLUE ROSE

When putting together this collection of stories, I did not want to just 're-gender' well-known stories. That would be too easy. But here, I make the exception. 'The Blue Rose' has a well-trodden path as a traditional story, and yet somehow, changing the gender of some of the characters suddenly gave it new life and explained just how wise and caring the emperor truly was.

The old emperor was becoming weary of this world. The burden of his years weighed heavily on his shoulders and he was ready to join his dearly beloved wife in the afterlife. He had worked hard to make China a happy and prosperous nation. His eldest son was married and already had sons of his own. The lineage would continue. He had only one wish: to see his youngest daughter settled and married.

As any good parent knows, one should never have favourites, but he did love this young woman. She was fierce and brave, beautiful and educated, and they spent many happy times together playing chess while discussing philosophy and religion.

And so it was, with her blessing, that he decided to find her someone.

An official decree was sent out saying that the emperor's family were looking for the perfect match for the princess, someone who could bring joy to her life, someone who would feel able to join the royal family. Suitors were to come to the palace to ask the emperor for the hand of the princess – but they must also present her with a perfect, blue rose.

Many sat up when they first heard the proclamation. Who wouldn't want to marry the princess and become part of the royal family? But a blue rose? China was the land of the rose, but whoever had heard of a blue one?

The chancellor saw his chance to become a permanent part of the dynasty and so straightaway he approached a successful merchant whom he knew could source most items.

The merchant listened to the request and said it would be no problem. 'If it is available, I can lay my hands on it. But it will take me three days to procure such an unusual item.'

The chancellor was anxious as to whether someone else would swoop in more quickly. But he realised it was an unusually difficult merchandise and grudgingly agreed.

The following morning, during the usual hustle and bustle in the emperor's throne room, after all the petitions and requests and arguments had been dealt with, the chancellor was horrified to see the captain of the guard step forward, bow low to the emperor and formally announce, 'Your Majesty, I have come to ask for the hand of your daughter.' And in his hand, he held something covered by a silk scarf.

The captain of the guard, a brusque man, accustomed to getting his own way, had also decided the princess and all that came with her would be his. The night before, he and twelve armed men had saddled their horses and galloped for the border into a little country that neighboured China. The captain had once worked for the young king of this country and knew that he was not a lover of confrontation. More importantly, he knew the king was a collector of fine artefacts and if anyone possessed a blue rose, then surely, he would.

The captain stood before the young man and made his demands. The royal guards stepped forward to protect their king, but he held up his hand to stop them, signalled to his chief minister, whispered in his ear and the minister bustled away.

The two men had once been lovers but had parted on bad terms. Now the king was aware of the captain's subtle threat to expose their secret.

There was an awkward silence as the young king simply smiled at the captain and eventually the chief minister came back with something balanced on his hand, covered with a silk scarf.

'Here. You served me well and although I don't appreciate your veiled demands, this may be what you are searching for.'

Now, back in the emperor's palace, the captain pulled away the scarf with a flourish. There in the palm of his hand was a beautifully carved sapphire rose. The palace onlookers gasped with astonishment. The chancellor groaned.

The emperor signalled to his daughter, who carefully lifted the blue rose from the captain's hand. She felt the weight, she held it to the light, she covered it with her other hand and smiled.

'I thank you for your marriage proposal, and for this beautiful blue rose, but I am afraid, for me it is not perfect. This rose is skilfully carved and has an enchanting hue of blue, but it is merely a hard rock fashioned by a craftsman. I look for something softer and gentler.'

She bowed low. The captain of the guard was furious and looked at the emperor, but the emperor simply shrugged, 'It is my daughter's decision.'

The captain turned and strode out, and the chancellor sighed with relief.

But he wasted no time. The next morning, he rushed to the merchant to demand that he find a blue rose by the next day. 'Of course,' said the merchant. 'When have I ever let you down?'

That very morning, again after the noisy business of the throne room, the keeper of the royal treasures stepped forward. The chancellor slapped his hand to his head!

'Your Majesty, I have come to ask for the hand of the princess in marriage.'

Again, the emperor signalled to his daughter, who stepped forward and bowed.

'And the blue rose?'

Now, the keeper of the royal treasures really did love the princess and had observed her many times around the palace. He felt that he knew her well and had found something that he was sure would captivate her.

He knew that the princess loved tea and he proudly presented her with a beautifully delicate, white bone china tea bowl with a transparent rose outline painted on it.

As the princess held the bowl carefully, he quietly clapped his hands and a servant came forward with a teapot. As the hot liquid filled the bowl, the onlookers gasped as the outline of the rose turned blue.

The princess looked at the bowl and sipped the tea, and as the liquid was drained from it, the bowl cooled, and the blue rose gradually faded.

She again bowed and said, 'I thank you for your marriage proposal, and for this beautiful blue rose, but I am afraid, for me it is not perfect. The blue rose was delightful in the heat of the moment, but it faded in the shortest of time. I search for a blue rose that will never fade.'

She bowed low once again.

The keeper of the royal treasures held his head high and strode out of the throne room. The chancellor sighed with relief.

Back at the merchant's house his wife found him doubled over with his hands over his face, weeping.

'Whatever is the matter, my husband?'

He told her the whole story of promising to find a blue rose for the chancellor, that he was coming the next day expecting him to have found one and how, for the first time, he had failed in his endeavours.

His wife thought for a moment and then said, 'Go to the apothecary. He is a man of science and magic, surely he can help?'

And so he did. The apothecary smiled and went to the shelves at the back of his little shop and came back with a little vial of red liquid.

'Take this vial home, but be careful. It is deadly poison. Choose a white rose in bud, cut it with a long stem and carefully place the cut stem in this liquid. The rose will drink the red poison and in doing so, by the laws of nature, it will poison its system and turn the opening rose blue.'

The merchant was astounded by the knowledge of the apothecary and gratefully paid him. He went home and with the help of his wife he carefully prepared the experiment. To their amazement, next morning, just before the chancellor was due to arrive, the rose turned blue!

The chancellor was delighted and paid the merchant well. He noticed that the merchant was being careful how he handled the rose and that he wound a silk scarf around the bottom of the stem to cover the poisonous thorns, to make it easier for the chancellor to carry it.

The chancellor hurried to the palace and arrived just as court business was coming to an end. 'Your Majesty, I have come to ask for the hand of the princess in marriage!'

The emperor beckoned to his daughter who dutifully stepped forward and bowed.

'And the blue rose?' asked the emperor.

The chancellor, with obvious care, produced the blue rose from behind his back and gave it to the princess, making sure she took it by the part of the stem wrapped in the silk scarf. She held it at arm's length and looked at the strange flower. The red poison had worked its 'magic' so well that the stem, complete with leaves, had turned blue, too!

The princess looked at the rose but, not wanting to offend her father's dear and loyal chancellor, said, 'I thank you for your marriage proposal, and for this beautiful blue rose, but I am afraid, for me it is not perfect.'

A few dead leaves fell from the rose as she spoke.

'This rose has no perfume, no creature will settle on its bloom and its life will be short. I crave something more pleasing in fragrance, long lasting and more natural to me.'

The chancellor nodded his head to her and then to his emperor, and bravely took his usual place just behind the emperor's throne.

The search for a blue rose had made for big news throughout the country. By now many visitors had made their way to the palace to see the fun when the princess made her choice. Street vendors and entertainers had set up in the city to entertain and make money from the visiting crowds. The whole city was awash with people and noise well into the night.

But that night, when the noise had begun to quieten, a musician from a troupe of actors began to play delicious music. The delightful sound filled the air, and everyone fell silent to listen to the beautiful, lilting sounds. The princess, in her apartment just above where the entertainers had set up camp, came to her window to listen and the music struck a chord in her heart. She made her way down her private stairs and hid in the shadows of the high palace walls, watching and listening, as this accomplished musician moved expert fingers over the strings to make such exquisite music. When at last the music faded and the silence seemed to make the whole world sigh, she beckoned from the shadows to the musician to follow her up the stairs. That night, they made sweet music together.

Before the sun began to rise, she whispered into the ear of the musician and as day broke, too soon, she was once again alone in her bed.

That morning, after the usual hustle and bustle of the court business had just about completed, a simply dressed musician stepped forward and stood before the emperor. All went quiet as the court and the emperor waited for her to state her business. She put her instrument bag on the ground, bowed and said, 'Your Majesty, I have come to ask for the hand of your daughter in marriage.'

The silence in the throne room was deafening.

The emperor beckoned his daughter forward and she bowed low.

'And the blue rose?' asked the emperor.

The young musician bent down and opened her bag and produced a long-stemmed white rose, which she had picked from the emperor's own garden before entering the palace. She gave it to the princess and bowed low again.

The princess took the rose and held it in her hands. She held it close to her face and smelled its perfume and felt its soft petals against her cheek. She rotated it in her hands to look at it more closely and pricked her finger on one of the thorns. She smiled and licked the little dot of blood from her skin. She sighed.

'I thank you for your marriage proposal, and for this beautiful rose. It is the most beautiful blue rose I have ever seen. If you will have me, I will gladly accept your proposal.'

There was uproar in the throne room. The chancellor, the keeper of the royal treasures and the captain of the guard all angrily stepped forward shouting along with the rest, but the emperor quickly stood and with a gesture of his hands, silenced them all. Well, nearly. The three angry ex-suitors still managed to mumble, 'It's not blue ... not of noble birth ... not even ... a man!' But the emperor silenced them.

'My daughter has made her decision. She has decided that this is the most perfect blue rose that she has ever seen. Who am I – who are we – to contradict her opinion, her choice?' He smiled at his daughter and declared, 'I am in total agreement with my daughter and I can see that this will be a wonderful marriage of like minds. Let us all prepare to celebrate and be joyful!'

And celebrate they did. The marriage day was filled with joy and laughter, and crowds turned out to see the emperor's daughter joined with her perfect blue rose.

When the celebrations were at last over, the happy couple slipped away to start a new life together in a little blue palace down by the side of the sea. They lived there happily ever after, and I am sure they made sweet music together for many years.

3

THE WATCH

I love the idea of lives and indeed stories colliding in that serendipitous way that they sometimes do. This is based, in part, on a true story.

Anita ripped out her earphones. Fumbling, she switched off the music and stuffed everything deep into the pockets of her black, heavy woollen overcoat. She smiled and nodded apologetically to the others sitting in the waiting room. Obviously her loud, if muffled, music had made them all turn to look at her. She made her way to an empty chair and sat down, wishing that she had not made such an entrance. After a while she ventured a quick look at all the other people in the room: mostly couples. Why was she always faced with couples? She sneered inwardly.

She couldn't help returning to it, but she would have been sitting as part of a couple if it hadn't been for Matthew. Matthew, the love of her life. She couldn't help still being bitter after all these years. They had met at university, were an odd couple, but somehow they seemed to fit together. After graduating they'd decided to set up home together, even talked about plans for the future, a business.

And then she had used his laptop one night, discovered what he had been looking at, why he spent so much time working on it. When she confronted him, he didn't deny it, confessed to everything and more, went upstairs, packed his bags, said he was sorry and then went. She had been left in a daze with no opportunity to talk to him about it, stunned with the speed of this – he was gone from her life.

Life became grim without him. Anita's plans for a career in theatre went out of the window, the wind knocked totally out of her sails. Instead she went down the temping route. Grim indeed.

Most of her work was in the city, and she was good at what she did, so work was constant. She began to neglect herself, had no social life, ate poorly and drank ... and that was how she had met dear George. She wondered if he had known that he, probably, literally, had saved her life. Dear George.

She had got into the habit of calling in at the wine bar, near the station, on her way home from work. She sat in the window, her earphones in, listening to tracks from her beloved musicals, with a large glass – well, glasses – of wine and one furtive eye on the clock so that she didn't miss her train home. Olives or peanuts became her evening meal.

One evening, she was sitting on her usual stool, miles away in her music, when she noticed a man standing next to her, miming an enquiry about whether the stool next to hers was free. She nodded and carried on listening to her music, but then, feeling a tinge of guilt at her rudeness, removed the earphones and said, 'Sorry, that was rude of me. I just get so engrossed.'

He raised his hand, 'No problem, no problem. Don't let me disturb you.'

But his smile captivated her. Pushing her phone and earphones deep into her pockets, she finished off her wine and said, 'I'm Anita. I have to dash in a minute, train to catch.'

'Ah, I see, yes. Don't let me stop you.' He proffered his hand. 'I'm George.'

They shook hands and she noticed that he was older than she had first thought, but he had such a lovely smile, and kind eyes. He stood when she stood. Wow!

A few nights later, George appeared by her seat again. 'Hello again. I'm a little earlier tonight. Are you here every night?'

Her eyes opened wide but then she realised he was teasing her when his face broke into a huge wide, crinkly grin.

'Please, can I get you another wine?'

It seemed rude not to say yes.

And so began their 'relationship'.

She *was* in there every night, and he appeared most nights too. They sat together, talked easily about music, theatre, the weather ... life. They drank wine together, laughed and became friends. But they never talked about their personal lives or asked each other personal questions. She had noticed that George wore a wedding ring and she had picked up from various things he had said that he had only recently married and to someone much younger. But she didn't need to know any more and she certainly didn't want to tell him her sorry story about Matthew ... because even though it had been a couple of years, there had been no other man.

One evening, he was there before her. He waved over to her and she joined him on the stool, glass of red waiting. They had become kiss-on-the-cheek-type friends, but everything was proper; George was a gentleman. So she was taken quite by surprise when he said that he had something for her, and he gave her a small, slim box.

She frowned at him questioningly, but he said, 'Oh, it's nothing much, honestly.'

She opened the box to find a rather funky, and very 'on trend', purple watch.

'I noticed how often you look at the clock, so you don't miss your train ... I thought this might help?'

She laughed. 'I haven't owned a watch for years. But this is too much.'

He explained that he owned a jeweller's shop, and that these were some watches that he had over-ordered.

'It's not an expensive one, don't worry. Not that I'm cheap!'

They both laughed at that.

It was on the same evening that George said he had a question that he hoped she wouldn't mind him asking her. She grimaced.

'No, don't worry. It's a bit of a confession really. I'm worried that I've been drinking a little too much recently. There's a nice café over the road, and I think I ought to frequent it more, rather than this delightful wine bar, but I wondered if we could still meet there?'

Anita enjoyed their evening get-togethers and so she happily agreed.

It was only later that she realised that George was really thinking of her. He'd noticed that she was drinking a lot and had guessed she probably wasn't eating too well either. This simple ploy of changing venue enabled them to drink coffee, water or fruit juices and eat something too.

She still enjoyed their meetings and made a point of checking her beautiful purple watch every now and again, but realised their friendship was just that; friendship.

Her friendship with George had begun to affect Anita in a positive way. She wasn't drinking as much, was eating a little better; but also, she had begun to take better care of herself and her appearance, and to think of the future.

One evening, she arrived early. She waited, looking occasionally at her beautiful watch, dying for him to arrive as she had a little gift to give him, but he never came – obviously one of the days when he didn't have to come up to town.

The next evening, she arrived first again but this time the waiter came over to her and spoke to her gently. He knew George because his jeweller's shop was just around the corner. He told her that George had suffered a heart attack and had not survived.

Dear George. If only he'd known what an effect he'd had on her. Now, in the waiting room, she looked at the purple watch, which she had discovered much later was in fact an expensive bit of kit, and smiled and thought of him. The coldness of grief that had welled over her was gone, and now, because of him, she was stronger and capable of facing many things.

Anita realised there were more folk waiting in the room with her, all dressed in black, and she scanned the room, wondering who they were and how they had known him.

The door opened and everyone stood, looking towards the door. She turned, and there was Matthew, after all these years! He came into the room and everyone smiled sympathetically and nodded, acknowledging his grief. The undertaker appeared and moved forward, hand outstretched.

Matthew reached out to take the undertaker's hand with both of his, and as he did so, Anita noticed his pale wrist against the black sleeve of his mourning suit. He was wearing a large, purple watch.

'I am very sorry for the loss of your husband, Matthew, but all your friends are here to support you.'

4

THE OGRE AND THE PRINCESS

I have been a little naughty with several faith tales here. Forgive me. The following story features in several traditions – Tamil, Persian and as part of the Mahabharat. Although it is an important part of much longer stories, it is almost glanced over in a few lines. I found it a delicious tale to rework and give new life to. I hope you approve.

The Yaksha was fiercely protective of his privacy. He didn't care for visitors; he didn't care to meet people; he wanted to live a simple life in the confines of his house on the edge of the forest. But being an ogre and a demi-god made that so difficult. Supplicants were always arriving at his door, asking for help or advice. It wasn't that he didn't want to help them, it was just that he didn't want to meet them face to face.

So, he had arrived at a subtle solution. When he heard footsteps approaching, he would crouch against his door and listen to whatever the worshipper was asking for and decide how he was going to help. Next, being a shapeshifter, and by reading their inner thoughts to find out what their deepest fear was, he would turn himself into whatever that fear was, and then answer the door. The supplicant would run away in terror, and although the Yaksha was in fact a very comely looking fellow, they would later describe him as a serpent, a spider or even their mother-in-law. The Yaksha lived a quiet life.

So, imagine how he felt when one day he heard louder-than-usual footsteps approaching outside, but when he read the visitor's mind all he could see was a beautiful young woman?! How could that be this supplicant's worst fear?

Intrigued, he opened his door and peeped out. In the near distance he could see horses and splendidly costumed soldiers, and there, standing at his door, was the very same beautiful young woman who had appeared in his mind.

'I am sorry to disturb your peace, oh great one, but could I ask for a few minutes of your time and your help?'

Without answering, the Yaksha opened the door wider and invited her in. As she swept by him, he felt the ripple of breeze from her flowing sari, inhaled her intoxicating perfume and heard the tinkle of bells from her silver anklets.

With a wave of his hand, a tasty buffet of sweetmeats and cooling drinks appeared, and he indicated to the young woman to sit on the couch. He sat at the other end.

She was obviously nervous.

'How might I help you?' he asked.

And so, she began to tell him her story.

'My name is Sikhandin, and my father is the king of Anga Dessa. I am his son! Yes, I know I am a girl, but please let me explain.'

'My father married my mother when they were both young. She was the first of several wives, but she was always his favourite. They had many children together, but each time she gave birth, it was always a daughter. At first my father was overjoyed but, as time progressed, he became more and more concerned she would never bear him a boy child to succeed him. After she gave birth to her thirteenth child, yet again a girl, my father took her to one side and explained his worries. He told her that although he loved her dearly, more than any of his other wives, he needed a son, and if she gave birth to another girl, the baby girl would be killed.

'My mother was obviously distressed, but being a queen, knew that my father was talking as a statesman, and she began to take actions that would ensure that next time she would deliver a boy. She prayed, gave gifts at the temples, spoke to priests, wise men and women, ate good food and took care of her body, and when she became pregnant again she was confident of giving birth to a son.

'But in the confines of her private apartments, with her women beside her, she gave birth to another girl. My mother and her women broke down in tears and wailed loudly. How could they allow such a beautiful baby to be put to death by my father, the king?

'Then, one of her oldest attendants stepped forward and said that she had a plan. She hurried along the corridors of the palace to deliver the news that the queen had given birth, and both mother and child were well. The king was excited and asked what sex the child was. He was overjoyed to hear that his wife had at last delivered a boy. He leapt to his feet, eager to see his new son, when the old woman stopped him. She told him that my mother had consulted many wise religious leaders while she was pregnant in order to ensure that she had a son, and that she had made a promise to the gods that if she had a son, the king would not be allowed to see the child until he married. The king collapsed in his throne at this news, but realised that a bargain was a bargain; the promise had obviously worked, therefore he must honour the deal.

'And so, I – the child – lived in my mother's apartment and was cherished and nourished by my mother and her women. My father kept his side of the bargain, but as he needed to ensure his "son" grew up to be a fine man, ready to follow in his footsteps as a future king, he sent teachers and soldiers to school me in everything I needed to know to flourish.

'The soldiers and teachers were shocked to discover that I was a girl, but were captivated by the story and this delightful child! They taught me everything I needed to know to be a future king and all swore allegiance and promised never to tell my father, the king, the truth.

'The years passed and I grew to marriageable age and my father decided it was time for his "son" to marry. Without consulting my mother or her women, he looked around for a suitable bride and, when one was found, he negotiated a marriage proposal that was readily accepted, by the king of *your* country!'

The Yaksha raised his head and sucked in his breath. He had heard about the marriage arrangements of the young and much-beloved princess.

'My father told my mother to make preparations for the wedding. He himself made preparations for the dowry and the journey, and without any further discussion I was sent on my way towards your country, and marriage to a princess.'

'And how can I help?' asked the Yaksha.

'Well, if I arrive as a woman at your king's palace, he will no doubt be incensed and will probably declare war on my father for the insult. I could bind my breasts and dress as a man, but I do not think that would be convincing. No, I have to be a man.'

And suddenly it all began to make sense to the Yaksha, why this beautiful young woman's greatest fear was that of a beautiful young woman!

'I have heard of your kindness and your great powers and I wondered if you could make me a man – if we could swap sexes – if I could become you and you become me?'

Sikhandin was extremely anxious and shifted her position on the couch. As the princess nervously shifted, her sari billowed and some of the delicious silken material fell across the Yaksha's hand. He rolled it between his fingers as he thought. The material felt comforting, the young woman's perfume calming, her story and her request beguiling.

'Of course, I will only need to be a man for a short time. Once I have won the love of the princess and we have married and consummated the union, I will be able to tell her the truth to persuade her that our life will be fulfilling together as two women and together we can approach the king. I will return here within seven days, I promise, and we can change back again.'

The young woman was so desperate and so hopeful. How could he refuse? With a wave of his hand, he became she and she became he. Each one of them looked down at themselves, and he smiled wryly while she let out an excited scream!

They both looked at each other.

'Oh, thank you,' she said and looked at him with such love in her eyes and their smiles turned to grins, then exploded into laughter.

You see, the now beautiful Yaksha was sitting with legs spread wide, struggling to keep the pallu of the sari on his head, while Sikhandin, now a handsome young man, sat with legs neatly together but her face wrinkling with the effort of trying to deal with her long moustache and beard.

'We both have much to learn before we venture into the outside world!' she said.

The outside world? The Yaksha considered that with relish.

And so began hours of lessons and advice. They stood side by side, in front of large mirrors, and both imparted pearls of wisdom on how to be a man, how to be a woman. There were lots of laughs, and even a few tears, but eventually both had mastered their new roles.

The Yaksha gracefully led Sikhandin to the door and they said their goodbyes.

'I promise I will return within seven days,' said Sikhandin, and turning, ran to his horse and vaulted into the saddle.

The Yaksha waved her hand. 'Good luck in your journey.'

She stood and watched Sikhandin and the soldiers canter off towards the city and the king's palace. When they had disappeared and the dust had settled, the Yaksha looked at the outside world, turned and closed the door to her house and strolled towards the village market.

Seven days later, the Yaksha heard approaching horses and a carriage. She looked out of the open door and saw Sikhandin dismount from his horse, leap on to the step of the carriage to kiss his bride and then turn to walk towards the door of the house.

'Welcome, my friend,' they both said to each other, and the two of them made their way to sit on the couch.

They looked at each other and smiled.

'I promised I would return within seven days, and here I am.'

But the Yaksha noted a little sadness in Sikhandin's voice.

'Tell me what happened,' said the Yaksha. 'You have never been far from my thoughts.'

'Well,' said Sikhandin. 'Everything went very well, as I had hoped. I was welcomed into the palace, the royal family received me well and from my very first meeting with the princess, it was clear that we were kindred spirits. The wedding was to take place five days later and most of the preparations had been completed. I had time to spend with my future wife and we became close very quickly. She is a wonderful person, well educated, spirited and has a love of life, very much like me. But as the wedding came closer, I began to have doubts. I knew it was not fair or kind to fool her into a marriage.'

'And so?' asked the Yaksha.

'And so, the evening before the wedding, I took her to a quiet place and I told her the whole story, the *whole* story!'

'And how did she react?'

'As soon as I had finished my story, I looked at her, and although there were tears running down her cheeks, she was also smiling. She held my hands and spoke softly but clearly. She would love me whoever I was. She could not believe how fortunate she was to have met such a kindred soul through an arranged marriage. It was a somewhat unusual situation, but we would get through it, together. But she said I *must* return to you to exchange sexes again, and if our one night of union was indeed our only night of union as husband and wife, that would be enough to last a lifetime. It was her suggestion to come here and see you first before we saw her father, and I agreed to be guided by her. Oh Yaksha, we are so happy together, and together I am sure we can conquer the world!'

Sikhandin looked at the Yaksha and smiled. There was something different, something almost radiant about her.

'And what about you, my dearest friend? How have you found the last few days?'

The Yaksha covered her face with her sari to hide her blushes.

'Oh Yaksha, what has happened? Do tell.'

And so, the Yaksha began to tell the story of the last few days. How the visit to the market on the first day had been so refreshing, and how she had been able to dress herself the next day, oil her hair and apply her make-up and enjoyed being out and about with the local people. And then on the third day ...

'Yes Yaksha, what happened on the third day?'

And the Yaksha told of how she had met a genie from the other side of the forest when she was in the market again, how she had come to his aid in a disagreement with a trader. The genie had been quite taken with her forthright nature and had walked her home. And he had called again, several times and yesterday –

'He asked me to marry him!'

Sikhandin sat back in his seat and gasped, 'Oh, how wonderful for you – is it?'

'Oh, don't worry – I too told him the whole story.'

There was a silence where they both looked at each other for a while and smiled.

The Yaksha stood at the door and watched Sikhandin run across the courtyard and leap into the carriage. There was no movement for a few seconds and then the young bride appeared at the carriage doorway. She gracefully stepped down into the courtyard and made her way to the Yaksha, where she knelt in front of her.

'I salute your grace and your sisterhood and thank you in the only way I know.' She took a beautiful gold and emerald anklet from her own ankle and fastened it around the Yaksha's ankle. 'We will be sisters from now on.'

The two hugged and smiled and hugged again.

The Yaksha and the genie had the most wonderful life together.

5

FIFTY SHADES
OF DORIAN

Here is a simple retelling of a classic story. I can in no way compete with Oscar Wilde's wonderful words, but I have included it in the collection for one main reason: I told the tale when I was storytelling to Spanish teenagers. The story concentrates on physical features and how they change over time, and these were key words the young people had to learn. We had fun as I drew a portrait of one of their classmates, with them telling me what facial features to draw. But it was also a chance for me to introduce the idea that it was fine to be attracted to both male and female friends, a concept that none of their teachers worried about me mentioning. It was also magical to see their faces when at the end of the story I revealed the portrait of Dorian I had drawn.

Dorian Gray was a young man of considerable charm and wealth. The only son of a wealthy family, his future was bright like a highly polished silver spoon. But, like a polished spoon and unlike a mirror, the reflection in the bowl of the spoon was never true to life. It reflected a reality that was distorted, contorted and disturbing.

In the beginning, his life took the obvious path of a young gentleman: fine clothes and food, only the 'best' of friends, good schooling and opportunity.

When tragedy struck, Dorian was left alone but fantastically rich. He presented an image of the grieving, deserted, desolate orphan to the watching world. In private, the satisfaction that he was now his own man granted him the certain promise of a world full of fruitful pleasures and unending gluttony.

Following a discreet but short interval after his parents' passing, he took stock of his position and his limitless possibilities. A planned career in the army was quickly dispatched and a life of a young gentleman-around-town was crafted. The country home was mothballed. Furniture and possessions were covered with dust sheets, like shrouds covering the dead, the staff were laid off, and he headed off for the gaiety and high life of London and a new life. *His* new life.

A suite at the best hotel was his initial home, and his excursions to the theatres and clubs of the capital announced to the waiting world that Dorian Gray had arrived, bright, glittering and endowed, and about to take society by storm.

Word spread speedily through the best and the worst of the glitterati, and within no time at all Dorian had created a wide circle of friends who were only too happy to help him live his life of excess. Women and men courted this new butterfly. Wings shimmering resplendent with bedazzling colours, Dorian flitted, alighting here and there, drinking all the pollen-laden pleasures that the city had to offer. But, unlike the delicate butterfly, Dorian was hard and purposeful, with a tough beetle-like outer shell. He knew exactly which of his newfound playmates could be trusted, which were there to help him celebrate his good fortunes, and which were there to feed, parasite-like.

Hotels find it hard to cope with debauched excess at the best of times, but with the torrent of guests visiting Dorian's suite being the sons and daughters of the high and mighty, the acceptable side of high society, it became difficult and challenging for hotel management. It soon became time for Dorian to move on. Certain friends had found him a house in the best area to rent and Dorian eagerly created the perfect bachelor household that he knew would be the envy of all. Opulent furnishings, works of art and large mirrors filled the many rooms on the many floors. Large mirrors to reflect the light, his fame and his likeness. A small, trusted gaggle of staff was employed to serve his every need. Lovers, male and female, frequented this palatial palace of pleasure as Dorian lived the life he desired, regardless of public commentary and gossip. He was beautiful and rich like the velvets he wore.

But there were fleeting lucid moments when Dorian took stock of his life and realised there was a future too that would follow this delicious present. He wanted to create something that would capture this moment, that would encapsulate all that he had 'worked' for, that would be a record of his life and status. Many would have planned a family with children to carry on the line. A wife and children would give him standing, display the upright character an older man should be craving, and he would be sure his wealth would benefit his progeny. But Dorian was not prepared to shackle himself to conformity. Life was for living. No, he would commission a portrait. A painting of himself, in all his finery, standing or lounging on a fine chaise. But there again, no, a portrait of just his face. Dorian was confident in his looks. His fine features had been commented on many times and the best portrait painters could reflect so much in the fine qualities and expression of a face, especially his face. He constantly had his mirrors to reflect his image; the world needed a painting.

And so it was that a series of sittings were arranged with a notable artist. Dorian sat on a chair, feeling high and mighty, glancing every now and again at a large mirror to the side of him, describing to the said artist just what was needed in the painting. The artist listened patiently, biting his lip, but listen he did, as this was a generous commission. Dorian described every facial feature that needed to be included as though the artist needed a prompt sheet. His bouncy, blond hair that caught the light from the window so enchantingly, his perfectly arched eyebrows, his forest-green eyes, his proud nose, lips that were full but not feminine, facial hair that was shaved and shaped to perfection, and his strong jawline. Oh, and the noble bearing of his head, his long neck, his ears – not too large – and his smile. The smile had to convey so much: benevolence and confidence with a hint of humility.

And so, over the next few weeks, the artist worked on a few sketches which Dorian pored over with great interest, until at last, the actual paint could be applied to the large canvas. Dorian sat whenever the artist worked on the painting, even though he had been told that sometimes the sketches were enough to work from. But Dorian needed to be there; the painting needed to be faithful and true, like staring into his friend, the mirror.

When at last the artist revealed the finished masterpiece, with more than a little trepidation, Dorian gasped with pleasure, almost tearing up at the beauty of the finished article. He gazed from painted image to mirrored, reflected image and stood tall. The artist was overwhelmed with the response but then had some difficulty explaining to his patron that it would be several months before the painting could be hung. Dorian was like a child waiting for Christmas, knowing exactly when the day was but impatient at every second.

At last the oils had dried and been varnished, the picture was framed and strung, and Dorian had his servants hang it high above the fireplace in the withdrawing room. The frame was polished until it shimmered and the chairs in the room were arranged to always face it. His friends and cronies gasped when it was unveiled, and Dorian feigned humility as they commented on and described the perfection of the painting and its astonishing likeness. He had to admit; it was a beautiful likeness.

Time passed, and Dorian noticed a change in his life. Slowly, members of his group began to form relationships that were consummated with marriage, and children were proposed. Even the rogues in the group began to visit less frequently. Dorian sneered in private at his group's pairings and spent his days wandering around the house, catching sight of himself in the countless mirrors and, of course, admiring his portrait. How could they all become shackled to family life, ships anchored with heavy chains weighing them down, slowing them down? But as time passed, Dorian realised that he too might begin to slow down, to age. He kept a close eye in his mirrors for greyness in his hair, wrinkles near his eyes. There was no sign yet, but the portrait? How could the portrait remain hanging on the wall, forever young while he would no doubt soon begin to show signs of age? The portrait would be mocking him and that carefully painted smile might, one day, show a sneer towards its owner, reminding him that he, the painted face, would remain forever young, while his master ...

Dorian could stand it no longer and, in a frenzy, he ordered his servants to take the portrait down. To wrap it in blankets, cocoon-like, and store it in the darkness of the attic, away from his sight.

Even more time passed. To society, Dorian was still a magnet. He was rich, single and beautiful, and although Dorian's original friends only visited when family life allowed, newer, younger, vibrant men and women fluttered round the dazzling light that was the Dorian Gray household. For many years, Dorian enjoyed this ever-changing, boisterous and youthful company, but there came a time when he found himself cringing, ever so slightly, when a late-night party or another visit to the opera was suggested. Late nights had begun to take their toll and mornings were increasingly greeted with the mirrored fear of signs of excess. But no. In the glittering mirrors that surrounded Dorian, there was no sign of ageing. Dorian noticed that his accomplices from the early days in London had begun to resemble the memories he held of his parents and their generation. Male friends began to have thin hair; some had gone bald. Wrinkles encroached on familiar faces and even shoulders began to stoop. Women friends seemed bloated, wore wigs and badly fitting gowns. Grey people living grey lives. Dorian looked at his perfect reflection in the mirrors and considered with horror that some of these creatures had actually shared his bed in years gone by.

But then the horror took on a new form, a new craziness. Why wasn't he ageing in his looks? It was true, he hardly ever attended late-night parties now, and he did feel growing signs of stiffness in his joints. Young men and women still found their way into his bed but never returned for a second visit, his youthful looks contrasting with his need for sleep. Life was becoming grey on the inside.

In panic, Dorian suddenly remembered the portrait in the attic. His likeness had been captured years ago on canvas and had lain there, in the dark, all this time. Surely, if viewed now, it would show some difference in the years that had passed? But that was the reason why the painting had been stored away; Dorian didn't want to acknowledge the passing of time. The worry and the indecision ate away at Dorian's mind. On the one hand there was the living proof of his youthfulness reflected in the mirrors and yet there was the memory of the painting again, of his youthfulness.

In a frenzy of passion, Dorian mounted the stairs, upwards towards the attic. Once at the door, hand on the handle, chest heaving from his emotions, Dorian calmed himself, took a deep breath and, turning the key, twisted the handle to open the door. In the gloomy greyness of the attic, he searched around and at last found the blanket-wrapped shape of the portrait. He frantically unwound the dusty shrouds and grabbed the frame to carry it over to the light of the small attic window. And in the light he stared, disbelieving, a scream jammed in his dry throat. For there in his shaking hands was the portrait of an old man with thin, lank hair, dull eyes and a face lined with wrinkles. The smile on the face was now tired and weary.

Dorian sank to the floor in misery. How could this be? In the dim light of the window, particles of dust floating magically in the air, the painting lay, thrown to the ground. Dorian slumped in the corner in the shadows, and a moan began to form in his throat. A moan, long and painful that gradually changed into a louder, protracted scream, bellowed around the house.

In Dorian's terror, his mind had cleared for just one second, and in that briefest of moments he was struck with the unthinkable. Now that he had unwrapped the portrait and revealed its magic, what would happen next?

But the thought could not be processed before his screams brought the servants running. Stopping at the door, they stood, frozen, hands on mouths, dumbfounded at the scene before them.

6

FROLICKING FUN WITH FAIRY STORIES

I woke up one night with fairy tale ideas whizzing around my head and had to get up and quickly note down all the craziness. Fortunately I was able to make sense of my middle-of-the-night scribblings and really enjoyed writing these three stories. Dare I admit that I laughed out loud while typing?

The Three Little Pigs

The builder's merchants had just opened their doors when the first customer of the day walked in. The First Little Pig (whom we will call the FLP) strode up to the desk and waited to be served. The rather imposing builder's merchant (from here onwards the BM) appeared and the FLP explained what he needed.

It appeared that he was moving out of the family home – it was such a pigsty. He had found a plot of land at the bottom of the hill and wanted to build a house but wasn't sure what materials to use.

Normally the merchant would have taken customers into the yard to look at the array of bricks, stone, wood, sand and gravel, but Health and Safety regulations had put a stop to that, so he produced a catalogue of said materials instead. He had begun to leaf through the pages when the FLP suddenly poked his trotter forward and stamped it on to the middle page. 'That's what I need,' he said.

The BM took a sharp intake of breath. Houses made of straw didn't stand up to too much weather. 'I would respectfully suggest that that is not a good idea, especially as at the bottom of the hill there tend to be strong breezes. One blow and the whole thing would come tumbling down. No, now what I would suggest ...'

But the FLP was adamant: this was just what he wanted. It would remind him of home, when the straw had been scattered around the sty and before it had been trampled into the mud.

Well, the customer is always right, so the BM sorted out for him just how much straw he would need to build a house, plus all the twine and wire clips to hold it together. The satisfied customer thanked him for his help, and walked out of the shop, happy that his order would arrive the very next day.

The BM had just finished entering the order on the company computer when the next customer marched into the centre. It was another little piggy, the Second Little Piggy (shall we call him the SLP?). The BM, who could see it was going to be one of those days, swept back his shaggy grey hair with his sharp claws, took a deep intake of breath and said, 'Yes sir, now how can I help you?'

The SLP also explained that he was moving out of the family home – far too overcrowded for him – and he had bought a plot of land halfway up the hill and was going to build a house for himself there.

The BM reached for the catalogue and flipped through the pages, when again, a determined trotter clamped down on a page and the SLP exclaimed, 'Perfect, that is just what I am looking for!'

The BM stretched his neck to one side with a crick, and again began to explain that sticks were not really strong enough to build a safe house, especially with all the sudden winds they had. 'All it would take is one huff or a puff of wind and the whole place could come tumbling down.'

But again, the customer stuck to his decision and the BM helped him fill out his order for the correct amount of sticks, twine and wire pins to build a house made of … sticks.

'I'm so excited,' said the SLP, as he skipped out of the merchants. 'A house made of sticks will remind me of the forest that I could see from the sty. Thank you, my good fellow, I look forward to the order arriving tomorrow.'

The BM watched him go out, thinking, 'Ah, but remember, forests can be dangerous places!'

Again, he had just entered the order into the computer and managed a quick swig of his tea, when the door opened and his third customer of the day waltzed in. This fellow made him stop in his tracks. What a confident and handsome chap he looked.

The Third Little Pig (you guessed it – the TLP) also took a gulp when he saw the imposing figure of the BM. What a tall figure he was, and he had such a soft spot for a fine, hairy chest. And those piercing, steely grey eyes?

He approached the counter.

'Now, you look like a pig who is going to set up home on his own and has come to order some building materials?' said the BM. He got out the catalogue.

The TLP said, 'Not sure how you knew that, but yes, you're right. But I do need some advice from someone with experience and I hope that you can advise me.'

The BM smiled at the TLP as he flipped through the pages to the back of the catalogue.

'And those white teeth,' thought the TLP. 'Such a disarming smile.'

Breaking their gaze, the two pored over the opened pages, and the BM pointed out their range of red brick and stone lintels. Sometimes paw and trotter touched as they both excitedly pointed to the perfect building material. A little buzz of electricity passed from one to the other.

The BM listened, entranced, as the TLP talked about the plot of land he had bought at the top of the hill where he wanted to build his house. 'Of course, it can get windy up there, so I need to build something sturdy. I don't want the first huff or puff of wind to blow the house down!'

The BM was in heaven. This was the kind of guy he had searched for all his life! 'It sounds perfect. I would love to see what you create.'

'Well come on up and see for yourself. Give me to the end of the week and you can have a look around and help me hang my etchings.'

'I will do. Thanks for the invite.'

They completed the order; the TLP thanked him for his help and wished him a good day.

The BM watched him walk out of the shop, and at the door, he turned and said, 'I'll look forward to seeing you.'

For the BM it seemed like a very long week, but he felt he had to stick to the agreement. After all, it would take the TLP a week to build his house, and he didn't want to appear too keen.

At the end of the week, he groomed his fur, picked out of his teeth a few scraps of spinach with a long, sharp claw, had one last look at himself in the mirror, brushed his bushy tail, grabbed the bottle of wine he had carefully chosen, a nice little blood-red claret, and went out the door.

He came to a house at the bottom of the hill and stopped, suddenly realising that this straw house must be the one built by the FLP.

'Good evening, how's it going, First Little Pig?'

'Oh, fine,' replied a hesitant voice form within, 'But I am not sure about the weather forecast for this evening.'

The BM was just reminding him of what he had warned – 'As I said, just one huff or puff and your house could blow down' – when a sudden gust of wind made the house of straw begin to shake. The gusts tore at the straw, the twine stretched and the wire pins pinged out of position.

The BM roared in his wolfie voice, 'Oh no!' The FLP gave a huge squeal and ran out of the back door just as the house came tumbling down. The BM watched the FLP run up the hill in terror.

'I did try to warn him,' he said sadly. But of course, the customer is always right.

The BM carried on up the hill, waving to a young woman dressed in a red hooded cape and carrying a basket of freshly baked cakes, when sure enough he came across the house of sticks built by the SLP.

'Good evening, how is it all going?'

'Oh, fine,' said a shaky voice. 'I'm glad I built it quite large as my brother seems to have suddenly moved in with me. But I am a little concerned about these gusts of wind.'

Again, there was a huge huff and a puff of blustery wind. The house began to shiver and shake and just as the BM roared once again in his gravely, gruff voice, 'Oh no!' the twigs began to creak, the twine began to twang, and the wire pins shot out like bullets in every direction. This time, two piggies ran squealing from the back door just as the house crumbled and collapsed into a pile of brushwood.

The BM watched as the two little piggies scuttled up the hill.

He sighed, gathered his thoughts and turned uphill towards the house of the TLP. And what a magnificent job he had made of it. It stood proud and strong at the very top of the hill. The red brick looked rich against the setting sun and the windows sparkled in the glowing light, edged of course with stone lintels.

He walked up to the front door and rapped loudly.

When it opened, there stood the TLP with a smile on his face. 'So good to see you, my fine friend, really glad that you made it. Slight change of plans though. The meal I cooked for us will have to be shared I'm afraid, as my two brothers have suddenly moved in with me. Don't worry, I am sure they will love you – no need to be nervous, they'll approve. They always like my boyfriends, and you look nice enough to bring home to meet Granny. Come on in!'

The BM sheepishly stepped through the door.

'And you have brought wine,' said the TLP.

Cinderella

I don't want to be critical of stepmothers, but her father's second wife and Cinderella did not exactly rub along well together. Understandable, really: two people vying for one person's affection, and new family members in the household exploring and defining new roles. But it didn't make for a happy household.

All Cinderella was concerned about was that her father was happy and that the house was looked after. But her new mum and sisters were not that bothered about housework, so it was left to Cinders, and she soon became known for her grubby appearance.

Cinders would have liked to have lovely clothes too, and to be able to sit in the garden reading magazines and drinking tea, but she had work to do. The house wouldn't stay clean by itself, nor the tea and meals miraculously appear; even the dog, Spot, needed walking. So she was usually found in the kitchen, wearing work clothes, working away.

When an invitation came from the palace, requesting their presence at the annual ball, it sent the household into a spin. Immediately, Cinders had the feeling she would miss out.

'Well, someone has to stay at home and look after the dog!' came the cry.

Cinders wasn't that bothered, to be truthful. She couldn't imagine having to spend the journey to the palace and the whole evening with the three, by now, demented women, and watch her dear father being henpecked.

'Spot and I will be fine, Father,' she said to her dear old dad as they all climbed into the family estate, large dresses and voices seemingly filling the vehicle. With a sigh, she waved them off.

But Cinders had only been back in the kitchen a few minutes when there was a swirling breeze, a swishing noise and a puff of smoke. There, standing before her, wand in hand, was, well, a large fairy. Cinders held on tightly to Spot's collar and tried not to guffaw.

'I know, all a bit predictable, but the manual says we have to arrive like this. Cough.'

Cinders invited the coughing fairy to sit on the chair and patiently waited to see what happened next.

'Now, I know that you were not too keen to go to the ball, but we thought that you should. Can't tell you why, but believe me, you should.'

Cinders smiled and thought of all the questions that she could ask, but decided not to. 'But I have nothing suitable to wear. And how would I get there?'

The fairy stood up and went across to the table. She picked up a long, large courgette and said, 'Follow me.'

Cinders dutifully obeyed and watched as the fairy bent over and placed the courgette on the drive, outside the kitchen door. She waved her wand, smiled at Cinders apologetically and suddenly the courgette changed into a shiny, green Corvette! Cinders was suitably impressed. With another wave, Cinders felt herself buffeted around.

When she stood firm again, she was wearing an elegant evening gown of peacock blue velvet with long sleeves, and she could smell the delicate fragrance of expensive perfume.

'I'm guessing my hair is wonderful too?'

'Oh yes, my dear,' said the fairy. 'You look stunning.'

'But I have to look after Spot.'

Another wave of the wand, a buffeted dog and there, sitting in the driver's seat, was a chauffeur, wearing dark sunglasses that looked ever so much like the dark marks Spot had over each eye.

'You shall go to the ball, Cinders!'

Cinders locked the house door and put the key into her gold clutch bag. She climbed into the car, next to the chauffeur, and the fairy began to close the door of the car.

'Have a wonderful evening, my dear, shine like only you can, but –' and she paused for dramatic effect, '– make sure that you leave before the palace clock strikes midnight, for after that magical time the magic ceases and all will be as before.'

Cinders looked at her with a frown.

'Yes, I know, a little dramatic, but all spells are monitored for training purposes, so I have to go by the book.'

Cinders smiled, blew a kiss and the car sped forward with Spot – I mean, the chauffeur – at the wheel. Spot was a remarkably good driver, although he did tend to slow down a little as they passed lampposts.

Her entrance was stunning – she was stunning, and the evening was stunning. The guests marvelled at her dress and hair, men swooned at the perfume, her new family looked green with envy, her father winked and acknowledged that he realised that the cool chauffeur leaning near the door was Spot, and of course, the prince was entranced by her.

He approached her with humility and asked if she would care to dance. And dance they did, all night. No other woman got a look in. If looks could kill …

But the prince held her tight whenever they were dancing, held her hand when they weren't, and held her glance whenever he could. He just could not let her go. When holding her close, she was aware of his care but also his hands occasionally stroking her bodice and shoulders. When he held her hand, with his other he stroked her sleeve. And when looking into her eyes, he occasionally dropped his gaze to her dress.

The time passed quickly. Soon Cinders realised that the palace ballroom clock said eleven fifty-five and she knew that the magic would disappear in just five minutes.

'Look, I'm really sorry, but I am going to have to go now. I've had a wonderful evening and I would love to see you again, if you don't think that is too forward of me?'

The prince took a step away from her and said, 'I am enchanted by you and would be honoured to meet you again. But must you go so soon? You look so wonderful in that dress. I really like that dress, I mean, I *really* like that dress.'

Cinders narrowed her eyes, laughed, kicked off her shoes, took him by the hand and dragged him up the ballroom stairs. As they passed the huge clock, she stopped, opened the glass door on the front of the clock and stopped the pendulum. She then grabbed his hand and rushed him upstairs to his bedroom. To his astonishment, she unzipped the dress and stepped out of it.

'Nice underwear, well done fairy!' she thought and then walked across to the prince. She stood in front of him and handed him the dress.

'I thought you were touching me a lot, but it wasn't just me, was it? It was the dress you liked too?'

'Yes,' he said quietly, putting his hands to his face to cover his shame, 'but honestly, I think I love you too. Please don't hate me.'

'Hate you?' said Cinders. 'How could I ever hate you? I've had a wonderful evening, and all made so lovely by you, well ... and a fairy, but mainly by you. I don't care two hoots that you like dresses. What I care about is that you're a real man. You know what you like and you should be able to live how you like – with me, if possible?'

They then spent the next few hours dressing the prince up in her evening gown and then exploring his secret wardrobe of gorgeous female attire. But it was no longer a secret from then on.

Cinders and the prince had fallen in love and they celebrated soon after with another ball, where the guests were invited to wear outfits that they had only ever dreamed of wearing before. The prince wore Cinders' evening gown and she wore a beautiful gold gown chosen from the prince's wardrobe. All the assembled guests could see that their prince had found love at last and rejoiced at his good fortune and his new love.

They were married that spring in traditional wedding outfits of a white lace gown and a white formal suit. Cinders was more than happy for the prince to wear whatever he wanted, whenever he wanted and wherever he wanted, during their happy married life that was blessed by three beautiful children.

The family photographs were always a delight to see too, usually taken by Spot, the family chauffeur.

Sleeping Beauty

Some parents just aren't good at making decisions, and sometimes it doesn't even help if they are a king and a queen ruling a huge and happy land.

First, when arranging the christening party for your beloved, long-awaited daughter, is it really a good idea not to invite the most powerful character in the land, even if she is called the Wicked One?

And then, when the said Wicked One does turn up to the party, wouldn't you apologise profusely and make excuses for why the invitation had not arrived?

And then, when all the other guests and fairies have given their presents of education, fairness, common sense, good manners, grace – oh, and beauty of course – you would not be too surprised, would you, when the disgruntled Wicked One, who has been left off the guest list and not given a very warm welcome, gives the child a present of a curse?

Now let us look at that curse. The horrified good fairies did manage to downgrade it from death to a period of falling asleep for a hundred years.

But what did her father, the king, do then? He didn't think about it in a considered way, did he? If he had, he would have realised that it is quite hard to prick yourself on a spinning wheel, as long as you are careful with the spindle (a literal spike that twists the fibre).

Instead of burning all the spinning wheels and then banning them from the land, wouldn't it have been better to send the lass to evening classes to learn how to use one correctly so that if she did ever find herself sitting at one (and remember, she is a princess with servants to do the spinning for her), then she would know how not to prick herself?

So, the young girl grew up in a land with no spinning wheels and lots of imported, therefore costly, fabrics. I bet the locals loved her for that.

Years later she somehow meets the Wicked One in a room at the top of a tower and is somehow encouraged to sit at the said dangerous spinning wheel and somehow, *somehow*, manages to prick her finger on the darned thing. You see? Yes, the princess has been blessed by all those wonderful qualities that have made her a fine and determined young woman, but that will all now go to waste because she didn't receive a little education on this matter of how to use a spinning wheel carefully, or even a warning about them.

So now we find the castle abandoned and almost derelict, surrounded by a veritable forest of brambles. Somehow the curse has dragged in the rest of the castle inhabitants, and everyone will sleep for one hundred years. That was a pretty powerful curse!

Over the following years, stories wash across the land, telling of the beautiful princess, asleep in her room, waiting to be awakened by a single kiss. I mean, who came up with that line?

And all those treasures lying around the castle and the possibility of battling your way in there, waking the princess with a kiss, hoping that she falls in love with you, that her protective father accepts you and allows you to marry her, seemed attractive to some. It was a tall order. But many young, and some old, tried. They battled against these barbed brambles that seemed to grow again so quickly whenever they were sliced by a sharp sword, blocking the way. Many men tried, many men failed, and many men unfortunately died in the process of trying.

A young woman, sitting on the hillside, caring for her flock of sheep, has seen it all before. She has shouted to many a man, 'Don't do it, look at all the dead bodies. You'll never be able to hack your way through. These are cursed brambles.' But most didn't heed her warnings and either perished or, after trying, came to her asking where the nearest hospital was.

And here is another one at this very moment, hacking away at the torturous wall of thorns, the decomposing bodies of other brave men, hanging, caught by the natural barbed wire of the curse, not discouraging him from at least trying. Maybe he will be the one?

She shakes her head as this one also gives up and turns away sullenly. At least he survived. 'Why don't they just think about it?' she muses.

She looks at the wall of twisted, barbed brambles surrounding and defending the famous castle but notices the rabbits, the badgers, even the bears, finding hidden tunnels to work their way into the brambles for safety or passage. 'It's so easy!' she laughs.

So she decides to prove it. She leaves her dog to guard the sheep and makes her way down the hillside. She walks around the wall of brambles until she spots an animal tunnel. True, it still looks difficult. There are tufts of animal hair caught on the brambles but no sign of dead bodies. And in she goes. Weaving and twisting, stopping and looking, turning and bobbing until at last she is through. And no, she doesn't meet a bear and get eaten on the spot.

Instead, she finds the main castle door and makes her way across the courtyard, stepping over dusty sleeping bodies as she progresses. The doors are heavy to open on their rusted hinges but at last she is at the bottom of the famed castle tower. She enters through the porch and begins to mount the stone steps up the tower. And there at the top, she finds the room and there stands the spinning wheel, covered in cobwebs. By the side of it lies the dusty and dishevelled body of the sleeping princess.

The shepherdess surveys the scene. What should she do now? She only set herself the challenge of beating those pathetic men to find the princess. Should she wake her up too? How will the sleeping princess feel when she wakes up, her body wracked with aching bones from lying on the floor, in the same position, for a century? And being woken with a kiss from a woman, not a handsome prince? That was no problem for the shepherdess, but it probably wasn't what the princess had been dreaming about all this time.

'Now, how would I like it to play out?'

Carefully lifting the dead weight of the young woman, she carries her to a bed in the corner and lays her on the soft mattress with her head propped on a pillow. She goes to the window and carefully picks a few sprays of bramble flowers and puts them on the bedside table. In a cupboard she finds a bolt of sheer silk and hangs it across the window to cut down the glare of the sunlight into the room.

'But there's something missing? Coffee! I can never wake up without coffee.'

She turns to the little kitchenette – well, it is a fairy story – lights a little stove and makes a strong cup of coffee and carries it with a steady hand, placing it on the bedside table. And then she pulls up a chair and sits by the bed and begins to gently hum and then to sing. She sings of ancient stories, of love, of battles to find love and of kisses, sweet enchanted kisses. And as she sings, and as the aroma of the coffee fills the room, so it must have filled the sleeping princess's head, for her eyes flutter open. She closes them again and stretches a stretch of a hundred years, and when she has finished, she turns her head to the young woman and smiles. She caresses the soft bed, so different from the hard floor that she has dreamed of. She looks at the little bunch of beautiful briar flowers that are so different from the cruel brambles that had twisted through her dreams. And she smells the delicious coffee, so different from the dusty dryness she had contended with while she slept. And she looks at the beautiful young woman, sitting close by, softly singing, so different from the bristly rude awakening she had dreamed of for so long.

'You did all this for me?' she asks.

'I would do this and so much more, in order to wake you from your nightmare and to allow you to live the life you deserve after all these years. To break the curse.'

'It is all so wonderful, and thoughtful too. But there is one thing that troubles me.'

The young woman anxiously looks around the room and tries to think what else she could have done to make the dawn of this beautiful woman's new life any more perfect.

'Don't look so troubled. It's simple. Please. It is just that I dreamed for so long that the curse would be broken, and I awakened, by a kiss on the lips.'

The young woman moves to sit on the bed and leans forward.

'Then let the curse be lifted and let us live the life we all deserve.'

And with this one, requested, sweet, gentle kiss on the lips of the princess, the world awakes.

And of course, they all live happily ever after.

7

CHRIS

I wrote this story from notes I made during a short-story-writing workshop. When I sat in front of my computer in my office at home, I had great fun working on the notes, creating story details, trying to add realistic intrigue, building character and researching the factual aspects. It seemed risky but worth adding to this collection and gives some insight into the progression of a new writer.

'But why?' is an often-asked question. Sometimes we receive an answer, satisfactory or otherwise, and at other times none, and we must deal with it.

We met online. He was much younger than me, by ten years, and after several days of cyber correspondence, we decided to meet up. A 'date' was arranged at a bar in town, a place I knew well and felt safe in. First dates can be scary, fun, boring or exciting, and the effort we put into them sometimes measures just how keen we are for them to work out. I put in a lot of effort.

Chris was just how he appeared on his profile. Strong in appearance and character, with a disarming smile. He greeted me with his usual opening line from our internet chats – 'Hi, handsome' – and a gentle touch to the cheek with his right hand. His eyes were piercing blue, honest and clear. I was suitably impressed, amazed that he would be interested in an older man like me and desperate to make the evening go well. I need not have worried. The conversation flowed easily, the laughter was loud, and any silences were comfortable.

Over the next few weeks we went for drives in the countryside, visited art galleries, drank coffee and got to know each other well. Friends were amazed and somewhat concerned when after a short time we decided to move in together, but it just worked; we were soulmates. And I knew I would never tire of his regular greeting of 'Hi, handsome' with its accompanying stroke of my cheek.

My family adored him and, being local, we had many family gatherings which did not faze him in the slightest. His family was another matter. It was a sad but common story: when they found out he was gay, he was no longer welcome at home. His only brother had protested but to no avail. Choices had to be made. To my good fortune, Chris had moved to Arizona to set up a new life. He still kept in touch with his brother, but generally, life in Chicago was left well behind him.

Life was good and we were a committed couple. Our jobs progressed well and our home life was blissful and so, after a few years when the law changed, it seemed an obvious step to commit legally to each other. There were, of course, romantic reasons for this, but also, being the older one, I was concerned for his future, and a marriage licence would guarantee it.

We decided on a low-key wedding and it was perfect. Obviously his parents would not attend but I had high hopes that at last I might meet his brother. But, after a long telephone conversation, it was decided no. He had recently moved to a small town between Arizona and Chicago and apparently he was tied up somehow.

We didn't dress in the same outfit; we had our own style and didn't want to look like twins. And included in his vows was 'Hi, handsome'. Perfect.

After a short getaway, life swung back to normality, whatever that is, and we progressed as man and husband. I was really pleased that the phone conversation to his brother before the wedding had stimulated more contact between the two of them and they now communicated regularly by email.

One day, when Chris arrived home from work, he didn't greet me with, 'Hi, handsome,' and there was no gentle touch of my face, a simple omission that was like a slap across the face.

We talked about the normal things, made dinner together as we always did and settled on the sofa to read and listen to music as we always did. But I felt as though I had been punched in the stomach. I caught myself staring at him. He smelled different, his smile was different somehow. And next morning, when we woke up, Chris said a cheerful, 'Morning,' and the day started as normal, but not normal too. There was no 'Hi, handsome.'

And so began a period of worry, of increasing panic and desperation. I might be imagining it, but was Chris now a little hesitant? Had he always allowed me to make the decisions, take the lead?

The age difference had always worried me. We had talked about it many times, but Chris had seemed not in the least concerned. His motto of living in the moment eased my mind. But now had doubts begun to creep in? After our years together, was he suddenly realising that the age difference was more noticeable? Was he having doubts? Or worse, did he have debts, was there someone else? *Was* there?

And the contact between him and his brother increased. They spent hours on the phone and I would watch Chris pace up and down the balcony, the glass patio doors creating a silent image, like an aquarium. But he told me little of their conversations.

I have never been a worrier, never overthought things, but all that changed. I became suspicious, on the lookout for any unguarded comment or action, any unusual suggestion or reason for being late home from work, anything different.

I fell into the usual traps. Emptying his pockets and looking carefully at receipts, hanging around whenever he was on the phone, listening into his conversations. Occasionally I took a sneaky peek at his phone and then one day I even considered logging into his computer. Perhaps the emails to his brother could throw light on my concerns. Oh my gosh, I was turning into the manic 1940s Hollywood film wife!

If only he would just say 'Hi, handsome', and brush my face with his hand.

The computer incident was the final straw, and I reined in my paranoia as best as I could. 'Normality' was the order of the day again. Live for the moment, for God's sake, live for the moment.

The following winter, Chris had to attend a two-week training event in Chicago. 'Chicago of all places! Chicago in winter?!' He was so grumpy. Why did he need to go? Why would they organise it in Chicago and why in the winter? But even he had to laugh when I pointed out the absurdity of his reaction. It was only two weeks and the training would guarantee him stepping up the ladder.

'I'll buy you a new coat,' I said. 'And then if you get really cold, you can snuggle down into it and think of me.' That's what started the laughter. But he held me to the new coat!

I guessed that he might be anxious about returning to Chicago, but there was little chance of bumping into his parents. The training event was at a hotel out of the city and a full programme of events was organised. I reasoned that he could be in any part of the world; corporate hotels were the same the globe over.

When his bags were packed and he was wearing his new and ridiculously expensive coat, we drove to the airport.

We had rarely spent much time apart in all the years we had been together, so two weeks seemed a long time. We waited in the busy terminus, arms around each other, watching the world. Businessmen, harassed mothers with screaming children, hordes of single travellers rushing around looking at information boards, scurrying official personnel consumed with security checks, labels and tickets. We stood together, clinging, an island of peace in this mad world. He seemed unusually edgy. He stared into my eyes several times and made as if to say something but then smiled and turned away.

'You okay?' I asked.

'Yeah, I'm fine. Flying. A bit anxious that's all.'

He'd never mentioned this before. I relaxed a little.

His flight was called, and we made our way to the gate. I passed him his bags and watched as, with the other travellers, he disappeared into the nightmare that is security and then on to Chicago, in the winter.

I expected at least a text message from him to say that he had arrived safely, but none came that evening. I went to bed feeling disgruntled but understanding that conferences and hotels can be hectic. He probably would realise too late and so put it off until the morning. But no. The next morning the phone screen was still empty.

I sent a simple message, 'All OK?' The answer came back nearer lunchtime, 'Fine, will message later.'

There was a bit of time difference. Perhaps he was in a lecture, or eating?

And that's how it continued. Short answers to my texts. Promises of phone calls that evening, apologies when they didn't happen. His room phone didn't work; he was having trouble with signal strength; they were working them hard. All feasible, possibly true, but bloody annoying.

By the second week, the anxious, frantic, doubting, quietly hysterical Hollywood wife arose in me again. Not attractive!

I phoned his work with some lame query about when the conference concluded and when I received the time and date, immediately felt guilty. Thankfully I didn't enquire if Chris was in attendance. No, he was busy; he probably had late lectures and workshops, he was drinking with other delegates, networking. That was why he was there, for goodness' sake. And so, I waited.

A few days before the end of the conference, I arrived home late from work and was annoyed to find a message from him on the home phone. Why hadn't he called my mobile? I pressed the button and sat on the arm of a chair to listen.

'Hi there. Sorry I've missed you. I've left the conference early, I'll tell you why later, but I'm having trouble getting back home. I've had to catch a train. Can you pick me up from the station at Winslow? The train gets in at about six thirty in the morning – sorry it's so early. Bad reception on my phone at the moment so probably won't be able to speak to you until I arrive. All will become clear when I see you, I promise. Hugs.'

Hugs? HUGS?!

Not the homecoming I was hoping for but if he needed me to get up that early and drive all that way to pick him up, then fine. But why a train? Not even a fear of flying would make me travel that distance by train. No one travels all that distance by train unless they are holidaying and stopping off at the many towns to see the sights. Thirty hours or more? I knew that mobile phone reception could be hit and miss when travelling by train, so I sent him a text that he could read whenever it reached him.

'Fine, I'll be there.'

The alarm went off at an ungodly hour. I shaved and showered, grabbed some coffee and toast and bundled into the car. I set the satnav for Winslow and followed the soothing tones of the automated voice to a place I had never been to before. Winslow was our nearest station on the Chicago-to-Phoenix line.

It wasn't a long drive but no matter. What else would I be doing this early in the morning? If Chris needed picking up, picking him up was what I must do. I suddenly realised that I was talking to myself through clenched teeth. I stretched my head and neck to each side and tried to relax.

It was quite a pleasant drive, but I wasn't going to admit that to myself. The roads were quiet. The hour and a half whizzed by and I pulled into the piece of stony wasteland that was the station car park. There was the slightest glimmer of morning breaking through. I was far too early, but I got out of the car and went to the entrance of the deserted and run-down station building. Apparently, the train from Chicago would be arriving on the side of the track with the waiting room.

It couldn't have been a more different scene from the airport I had dropped him off at. Dusty and deserted, lights struggling to compete with the rising sun and reminders of another age. Every door I tried was locked and there was no sign of a vending machine. I stood on the platform, the one with the waiting room, turned my collar to the chilly breeze and looked down the line. It disappeared into the distance in both directions with no sense of where it came from or where it led. It was still early and a little chilly, but I was obviously anxious as I felt a prickly heat under my collar. Signs swung in the breeze announcing comforts that were not available. There was a timetable against the wall protected by a sheet of Perspex that someone had helpfully spray painted, so the desired information was unavailable. It was six-thirty when the train was due, wasn't it? I looked at my phone. The signal was slight.

And then, just before six-thirty, there was action. Travellers began to arrive for their commute to work, some eating doughnuts or drinking coffee, others applying make-up using hand-held compacts. I suddenly felt guilty about my leisurely start time and journey to my job. In the distance came the haunting sound of the train whistle and, as though it were a Pavlovian signal, a guard appeared from a previously locked door. We stood back as the huge train pulled to a stop alongside the platform. The travellers rushed to various doors, opening them and climbing aboard as the guard walked officiously back and forth, looking up and down the train. For an instant I panicked. Then, to my huge relief, another door opened, and down stepped Chris, wearing the coat I had bought him. He turned to retrieve his luggage from the train doorway and then he stepped back, looking into the doorway. Down stepped another Chris! They both turned, luggage in hand, and faced me. They walked towards where I was standing but then the Chris wearing the coat stopped. The other Chris walked towards me, lifted his arm and placed his hand against my cheek.

'Hi, handsome!'

Those words I had longed to hear for such an age!

I felt my stomach churn and my chest thump. I looked into those beautiful clear blue eyes. In my peripheral vision I could see the other Chris standing back, stepping from foot to foot, with a worried expression on his face.

This was the Chris that I had met, mated and married and yet standing nearby was the Chris I had lived with, wearing the coat I had bought him to remind him of me.

And then in an instant it all fell into place. I had married one but lived with the other, and now they were both presenting themselves to me ... identical twins.

I lifted my arm, caught Chris's hand and tore it away from me.

'BUT WHY?!' I yelled.

'But why?' – an often-asked question. Sometimes we receive an answer, satisfactory or otherwise, and at other times none, and we must deal with it.

8

THE KINGDOM ACROSS THE SEA

Several years ago, I heard a wonderful Danish storyteller telling a set of stories that had been collected by a folklorist from women in the villages and towns of late nineteenth-century Denmark. They were all considered to be rather racy. One stood out for me. I decided to include it in this collection, but I changed it considerably. One part was too graphic, and the end didn't suit what I had in mind. Yet, having written it and read it through again, I suddenly realised that both versions could work. So, here is my version and at the end I'll tell you about the changes and the original ending.

Many years ago, in a kingdom across the sea, a beloved king lost his wife soon after she had given birth to a beautiful baby girl.

The king and the whole kingdom fell into a deep despair, mourning the loss of their young queen. Everything became grey, matching the late winter weather, but, as spring began to creep into the land, little touches of colour began to appear. The people realised that life must go on, and although they would never forget the queen, a kind of normality graced the kingdom once more.

The young king had a kingdom to rule, a people to take care of, diplomats to meet, decisions and appearances to make. He found that keeping busy helped to mask the pain and at least gave an outward look of normality.

But in private, he brooded. When he had so much in the world, how could this have happened to him?

His little daughter had many people to take care of her. Princess Alice was doted on by the servants and began to grow into a strong, brave and well-loved young woman, just like her mother. She had the same wavy hair, a skip in her walk and a merry laugh.

The king loved his daughter, but the older she got, the less time he could spend with her, she so reminded him of his beautiful wife. It was too painful. And his daughter recognised this fact. When she looked in the large palace mirrors, even she could see the resemblances. How did she know? Well, at the top of the stairs there was a life-size painting of her mother that had been created soon after her marriage to the king. She was still very young, beautiful and proud, and she was wearing the dress she had worn at the ball held to celebrate their wedding. It was an image that seemed to haunt the halls of the palace. The servants would try not to stare too much if they happened upon the Princess Alice near the painting, and her father just could not look at his daughter as she grew taller and began to blossom into womanhood.

The queen's chambers had been left just as she had left them. They were regularly cleaned and maintained but because the king never married again, there had never been a reason to clear them out.

The king spent more and more time in there. His servants were too respectful to disturb him, but all had noticed that over the years, the muffled cries that had emanated from the room in the early days had changed to an eerie silence. And all had noticed how the young king had aged quickly. Grief affects us all in many different ways.

From a small child, Alice too had spent much time in her mother's rooms. It felt safe there, comfortable. The servants had tried to stop her, but her father had said, 'No, leave her be. Let the child get to know her mother.'

But by some strange quirk of fate, the king and princess had never been in the rooms at the same time, until one evening.

Alice was a strong-willed child who would not be coerced into wearing courtly dresses if she didn't want to. Nor would she be shushed if she wanted to say something.

And nothing could stop her crying or laughing, if she was so moved. She missed a mother's love; she missed even her father's. Why was it he couldn't seem to even look at her?

One afternoon, while rummaging deep in the queen's wardrobes, she came across a beautiful, flowing evening gown. It was deep green and made of the richest silk she had ever felt. She took it from the hanger and held it in her arms, inhaled the musty perfume and, holding the dress like a shroud in her arms, she sat on the floor of the large cupboard. Why did this dress seem so familiar? The feel of it? The smell of it? It brought to her mind such a strong image of the mother she had never met, but why?

And then she realised. Leaping to her feet, she ran to the top of the stairs. Of course, it was the dress her mother was wearing in the painting, an image so familiar to her that this dress *was* her mother. And a crazy idea came to her. She looked carefully at the painting, taking in every detail she could, then ran back to the rooms and laid the dress on the queen's bed. She then began to search the dressing table, the drawers, the boxes and bags until she found everything she was looking for. She sat in front of the dressing table mirror and began to apply her mother's make-up. It was dry and dusty, but a small amount of spittle helped encourage it back to life. She took the comb and brush and began to fashion her hair in the same style, pinning it back with bejewelled hairpins. She stood back from the mirror and quickly removed all her clothes, stepped into her mother's matching satin court shoes and then turned to the bed. The dress felt cool against her skin as it slipped over her arms and dropped into place around her body. Young, agile arms were able to reach behind to fasten the hooks. She managed this all alone with no servants or ladies-in-waiting to help her as her mother no doubt had employed. The dress fitted perfectly.

She stood looking at herself in the mirror, smoothed the silk out and smiled. Oh, how she would have loved to have run out into the palace to show everyone! But she knew not to. As she looked at herself in the mirror, her brow furrowed a little. Was there something missing? The musty aroma reminded her. She leant forward, picked up the crystal bottle and gently applied the perfume to her neck and wrists. She placed the bottle back on the dressing table and was just giving her wrists a final rub together when she heard a loud and distressed gasp from behind her. She did not need to turn around. She could see her father sitting on the bed, his countenance white, his hands holding each side of his face in disbelief.

She didn't dare turn around but instead wailed, 'Oh, Papa, please forgive me?'

The king rose slowly from the bed and approached her. She watched his reflection in front of her and looked for the tell-tale signs of a shout or even a slap, but no. He simply stood behind and looked at her in the mirror. The king smiled slightly and she saw him tilt his head to one side as he looked at her. He gently stroked her hair, he placed his hands on her shoulders and then down on to her waist. He moved slowly closer to her and, brushing the curve of the side of her neck with his mouth and nose, inhaled the perfume and deeply sighed. She relaxed inwardly.

'Oh, Papa, are you pleased?'

But then Alice began to feel uncomfortable, not because he was hurting her but because her father had never been so familiar with her. He had never held her, sat her on his knee or kissed her goodnight as most fathers did. As his hands slowly slipped further up the curves of her sides, tears began to well in her eyes. She struggled a little and suddenly the gentleness of the hands turned into a firmness of passion. She felt his strong hands cup her young breasts and she cried, 'No, stop!'

But in her father's mind, he was with his passionate young wife, and his grip tightened on the body that he had missed and yearned for.

In desperation Alice again yelled, 'No!' and instinctively bit into her father's wrist, making him let go of her and fall to the floor.

She turned and ran to her own rooms, for safety.

She slammed the heavy door shut and bolted it, then went to her mirror and looked at herself, face tear-stained, eyes wide and hair wild. What had just happened? Why had her father done that to her?

She began to rip the hair pins out of her hair with one hand and rip the dress from her body with the other, not caring that the dress would be ruined, ignoring the trickles of blood running down her face from the roughly scrabbled-for hairpins. Standing there naked, she scrunched the dress and began to rub frantically at her face and neck to remove all trace of the make-up, all trace of the perfume, all trace of her mother and all trace of her womanhood.

Flinging the dress to the ground, she looked at her frantic and bedraggled reflection in the mirror and saw her breasts and they disgusted her. In one frantic minute of madness she snatched her little hunting knife from the table and, holding one of her breasts firmly, she hacked into it with the blade.

She must have collapsed from the pain and sudden shock from what she had attempted. As she lifted her head from the floor, it was several seconds before she remembered where she was. She was cold from lying there so long and when she slowly lifted herself up, her hand quickly went to her breast with the sudden stab of pain, the feeling of the sticky, warm blood making everything come flooding back. In panic, she dragged herself on to the bed. She lay there gasping, wondering how long she had been lying there, why her father or his servants were not beating the door down. It was dark outside, but Alice knew she had to get away. Her father, indeed, no man, would ever treat her like that ever again.

She tore up some sheeting and bound her breasts tightly. Running to her closet, she grabbed her hunting clothes and quickly covered her nakedness. She filled a small bag with some possessions and finally, threw a huge hooded cloak around her shoulders. As she made for her private entrance, she noticed one of the bejewelled hair pins on the floor. Not understanding why, she bent, picked it up and threaded the long pin in and out through the edge of her cloak. Then, pulling the hood over her head, she ran down the back stairs and out into the castle courtyard. There was a cold wind, but she was dripping with sweat. In the stable she quickly saddled up her horse, led it out of the side gate, mounted and galloped for the forest, never once turning to look back at the life she was leaving behind.

Her mind was full of turmoil and questions. Was this how men treated women? Is this how her father treated her mother? And she galloped on, deep into the darkness of the trees of the forest.

As she galloped, the heat inside her cloak became unbearable. She flung the hood back, but it made no difference and she had to stop and dismount by a stream. She staggered over to the bank and drank, cool water. But a fever was on her and she collapsed in a heap in the frosty grass.

She had no idea how long she had been lying there, but when she woke, the sun was high and the wind had ceased. She sat up and looked around. Her faithful horse was munching grass close by in the shade of the forest trees. The pain in her chest was fierce and she lifted her tunic and peeled away the bloody bandage, exposing the deep wound. She bathed the wound with the water from the stream, its coolness easing the throbbing, and calming her own inner heat. From the little bag she pulled out more of the ripped sheet she had stuffed in for later, and again, tightly bound and wound it around her body, easing the pain and flattening her breasts. A thought came to her and she rummaged in the bag and pulled out the little hunting knife, swished it around in the stream water to clean the blood from it and then hacked her flowing locks of hair off close to her scalp. She threw them into the stream and watched the current sweep her woman's hair away. From now on, she was a boy.

She led her horse through the trees, not knowing where she was going or what she was expecting to find. After some time she smelled woodsmoke and came upon a little house among the trees. An old man sat on a stool by a fire.

'Hello sir,' she said.

'Hello,' said the old man, not looking up. 'Are you hungry, would you like some stew?'

'That's very kind of you.' Alice sat down on another stool and waited to be served.

'What shall I call you?'

'Al ... Alan,' said Alice.

'Well then, here's a bowl and spoon. You can serve yourself.'

The old man felt around and finally found a bowl. 'Alan' realised that the man was blind. He helped himself to stew and quickly ate it up.

'You do seem hungry. There is plenty in the pot, take some more, my boy, and put some in for me too.'

The two of them sat and ate and when they had finished, Alan stood to leave.

'You're not going to leave so soon, are you?' asked the old man. 'My granddaughter is away and won't be back for a week or two. Would you mind staying and keeping me company?'

Alan smiled with relief. Time, rest and company was just what he needed – and in the company of a blind man too!

'I suppose I could stay a little while,' he replied.

Over the next few days, Alan slept a lot, ignoring the old man's comments about how much time he spent in bed. He ate a lot too, building up his strength. When he could, he took himself privately to a stream and bathed his wound, always rebinding his breasts.

He enjoyed the old man's company and the old man seemed to like him too. He told him all about life in the forest. He had lived there a long time and his granddaughter, Fay, spent most of her time with him, looking after his daily needs. The old man talked about Fay fondly and Alan began to conjure up a picture of her in his mind. How he would like to meet her! But he knew this was not possible. Deceiving a blind man was easy but a young girl would soon recognise him for what he was. No, he would have to leave before she returned.

But Fay came back a day early.

'How lovely to have you back so soon, my girl,' said the old man.

'But Grandfather, you knew I was due to return today!'

She smiled at her grandfather and then at Alan.

'This is Alan. He has been keeping me company, and good company he is too!'

Fay smiled at Alan and curtsied slightly.

'Well, you are welcome to stay longer if you wish,' said Fay. 'We can always make use of a strong pair of hands around the cottage, can't we, Grandfather?'

'Oh, yes,' he said, nodding sagely.

Alan was not sure, but he seemed to have been accepted by Fay, so why not?

Over the next few weeks, Alan stayed with Fay and her grandfather, the three of them lived happily together. Grandfather was a fount of wisdom and a delight to spend time with, especially when he stared into the fire at night and told his stories. Fay was equally a delight. She was so capable; nothing about life in the forest fazed her and she had no real need of a pair of men's hands. But the two of them spent many hours together, working, cooking, and foraging for food and wood to burn. And laughing. Alan had never met anyone with such an infectious laugh.

He had to find time away from the house to nurse his wounds. He would go down to a pond in the rocky stream, remove his tunic and bandages and then, all the while looking out for Fay, he bathed his breast. And, in time, the deep wound began to heal. The physical wound, that is. At night Alan had dreams: not exactly nightmares, but dreams that made him talk in his sleep. One night, when he woke with a start from a dream, he found Fay lying in the bed next to him.

'Shhh,' she said. 'It's just a dream. Lie next to me, I will soothe away your worries.'

And she held him tight, her arms wrapped around him. He breathed quickly at first, the hold reminding him of his father, but soon he relaxed. There was something so caring about this hold, this embrace, and they were soon sleeping in the same bed each night, so she could be there for him.

But how could he allow Fay to fall in love with him when he was really a girl? And how could he deceive the old man any longer, when he had been so kind to him? Fay would soon find out the truth.

Once, while bathing, he caught sight of his hunting knife. Could he finish the task he had started all those weeks ago? No, that would be foolish. Could he tell Fay the truth? No, that would be equally foolish. If he didn't think of something soon he knew he would have to leave, but somehow *that* felt foolish too ... he knew now that he loved Fay.

One day he decided that he would have to go. Fay was in the forest collecting herbs and the old man was dozing. Alan quietly began to gather his meagre possessions together but, before he left, he decided to make one last visit to a place that had become a sanctuary to him over the past weeks: the rock pool in the stream.

He sat by the side of the water and dangled his hand in the current and all his worries began to wash away. He looked at the familiar rocks and overhanging bushes and then closed his eyes to listen one last time to the sound of the water, the rustle in the leaves and the birds singing. He was suddenly stirred by the voice of the old man.

'Don't leave her, lass! She loves you. We both do.'

Alan opened his eyes and there was the old man leaning on his staff, unseeing eyes looking in his vague direction. 'It doesn't matter to her. She loves *you*, not someone you think you ought to be!'

'But how can that be? How can I ever tell her? How can we be together if we are both women?'

'Why not just ask me?'

Alan turned sharply and there was Fay, standing on the other side of the pond. She walked round the edge to stand by her grandfather.

'How long have you known?'

The two of them looked at each other and said:

'From the beginning ...'

'From the first moment I saw you ...'

'But why didn't you say anything?' Alan asked.

Fay replied, 'We both guessed that you needed time. Time to feel comfortable, time to feel at home, time to feel loved for who you are.'

Alan stood up and walked across to Fay and the old man. And then the three of them walked back slowly to the cottage. Grandfather, Fay and Alice.

And, of course, they lived happily ever after.

In the original version of the story, the young princess slices off both breasts and, in the end, through the magic of the fairy tale, she changes from a girl into a young man. And the couple live happily ever after in the conventional sense.

I found the image of slicing off her breasts just too upsetting and was disappointed that two young women couldn't become a couple without one of them becoming male to fit the 'norm' of what an acceptable couple should be in society.

But then, it suddenly hit me that I was missing another huge tale. In the modern world, many adults do in fact go 'under the knife' in order to change gender, though thankfully in a more gradual and much less violent way. How foolish was I! So please, if you prefer this alternative ending, sit back, close your eyes and re-write this story in your own words: the story of a courageous young woman, transitioning from female to male, and of her full acceptance by society and her new partner and family. An equally powerful story.

9

GARY MEDE

The story of The Rape of Ganymede has always fascinated me, especially when I realised that the word 'rape' often means kidnap in classical translations. Here is a modern retelling of the story. How many classical references can you spot?

Living a lie. Three little words. Easy for some, devastating for others. *Living a lie.*

Zacharia Ida, known to all as Zee, had been a god in the world of football. The son of Greek immigrants, who had worked hard to build a huge business, Zee had been given every opportunity their newly acquired wealth could afford. Rubbing shoulders with the greatest in the land, and put through the best schools with an eye on an Oxbridge place, who would have thought he would become a professional football player?

But no ordinary football player. He was one of the first super players who arose in the eighties. With the right agent, obvious talent, judicious contracts all over Europe and a monied background, he had become lauded as one of the greatest footballers of all time, one of the most handsome and one of the wealthiest players ever.

Caps for England gained him national notoriety, but it was his looks and his wealth that put him in a league above his fellow players. And he was an all-round good guy to boot.

During his career, his agent Troy had guided him well. A high-profile wedding to a glamorous model, resulting in three beautiful children, all girls – including a set of twins, of course – had guaranteed him a future career in modelling, as a TV pundit and as a football agent. Life was good.

Throughout his public career, he and his family appeared many times in the glossy magazines and although this exposed, even flaunted, his golden career and glittering lifestyle to his adoring public, no one seemed to begrudge him all this. You see, he was a good guy, squeaky clean.

No, really, he *was* one of the good guys.

The years were kind to him too. He still had the dark, Mediterranean looks, combined with a healthy head of hair with just the right amount of grey in it, a flashing smile and, even though now in his fifties, the body of a Greek god. But it took a lot of work to look like that.

Among his many projects he owned an exclusive hotel and health spa, Catamitus, in the centre of London. It was a place he could live the lifestyle he was now used to, conduct his many business deals and keep his body trim.

His management company, Olympus, had fingers in many pies. Property was the main concern and Olympus had a portfolio of exclusive properties around London and, of course, in Greece. Whether it was a secluded and safe home, a prestige office block or a TV or film location you needed, Olympus, with Zee nominally at the helm, was the company to approach. Film stars, royalty, sportsmen and politicians approached this organisation because of its quality stock, connections and security; business was good.

But Zee was still obsessed with football. And now that his business was well managed by carefully chosen acolytes, he had time, and money, to spend on his passion, his ambrosia: developing a new Zacharia Ida.

He recognised the fact that his background had initially kickstarted his career. Even though his father had hoped his son would become a businessman like him from an early age, he did recognise his son's talent and drive to make it in football. His wealth and connections had made it much easier for Zee to obtain the best training and trials. Zee would never forget this and would never be able to tell his father just how much this meant to him. But he also knew that this was not the case for most young men. He wanted to pass on his experience, guidance and passion to young players. You see, he was a good guy.

Catamitus had developed training grounds and facilities for gifted players. Zee kept an eye on the teams in the lower leagues, scouting for promising, talented sportsmen, and when suitable players were spotted, Olympus would offer them bursaries, the chance to improve.

Many young men had been given that extra lift to boost their careers and many now played in the top clubs. That gave Zee great satisfaction. He was giving something back to the game. But Zee had never found anyone to become the new Zacharia Ida, that special person with incredible talent, the brightest and largest of personalities and the physical beauty, that he could help develop, mould and encourage to become the new him.

His wife, Hera, was as supportive as ever. Her modelling career lasted for some time; she graced the catwalks and magazines of the fashion world for several years after they married, but the children had changed her in too many ways. She too loved this good guy, and especially their children. Family life and her husband's career took over, and she was glad. She had never really enjoyed being placed on a pedestal, on constant view. She loved the stage-managed version of their family life that was presented in the magazines but was happy when the shoot was over, and she could go back to her own queendom.

Zee was aware of his age. He guessed he wasn't immortal, although he felt he could go on forever. Hera supported him in every way she could.

And then, during a visit to a football match at the university his youngest daughter had attended, Zee spotted him. A young player with incredible skill, who lit up the game every time he touched the ball: a player who seemed to have amazing individual skill but also a team player who was generous enough to share the action. This was it. Zee had to meet him.

Leaving Hera and his daughter to make their way home in the Rolls, he made his way down to the changing rooms. His name and face were obviously well known, and the coach was only too happy to escort him down to meet the winning team.

On the way down, Zee enquired about the young player who had scored the winning goal.

'Oh, Gary, Gary Mede. He's not been long with us. Great player. Lots of promise. And he's a good guy too.' The coach opened the changing-room door and steam and singing billowed out. 'Gary. Gary! There's someone here wants to meet you.'

The changing room fell silent when the victorious players saw Zacharia.

A young man with his back to the door, drying his long, tousled blond hair with a towel, turned to see who was there. His eyebrows shot up. 'Eh up mate, what are you doing here?'

Zee was struck by the sheer beauty of this young man: his disarming smile, the spark in his eyes and the tall, upright and toned body.

Zee handed him a card. 'Give me a ring on Monday, will you, lad? I would like my agency team to have a chat with you if you're interested.'

There was a huge and supportive roar from Gary's teammates who knew instantly what this invitation could possibly mean.

Gary seemed floored for a second. He cheekily stuffed the card down the top of the towel that was wrapped round his waist, proffered a grin and a hand and beamed from ear to ear.

'I look forward to hearing from you, then,' said Zee, nodding and then turning to exit. As he made his way from the changing room, he heard one of the teammates roar, 'Houston, the eagle has landed!' and the whole room erupted with cheering and singing.

Hera could sense the excitement in Zee when he returned home and for the rest of the weekend she was aware of him circling the large rooms of their holiday home as he paced in thought.

Back in London, on Monday morning, Zee listened in as one of his management team arranged for Gary to visit the facility in the middle of that same week. He was advised to bring someone with him to offer support.

And so, that Wednesday, Gary Mede, along with the coach from his current team, Colin, made the trip to visit the facility. They met with various members of the management team and a tentative offer was made to Gary, with the proviso that he passed the medical examinations.

Zee stood around while the negotiations took place on his behalf but then just happened to bump into Gary and Colin as they made their way to the medical suite. Zee feigned surprise at meeting them but after much handshaking and some gratitude from Gary and Colin, he hung around, talking to Colin, but watching Gary as he undressed and made ready for the medical. He certainly was a fine figure of a young man, making Zee even more confident that Gary could be the protégé he had searched for over the years.

'Tell me a little about him if you would? It's Colin, isn't it? It's good of you to attend with him, I thought maybe his father would have come too.'

There was an intake of breath from Colin and he explained, 'No, Gary's father left many years ago, when Gary was about twelve. Never had time for anything or anyone, did Gary's dad. Gambling problems. He would have let you have control over Gary for a sure-fire tip on a major horse race. No, Gary has done well with the support of his mother. Even made it through university. Discovered his talent for football in the university team. That's where we spotted him.' Colin looked at Zee with a grin on his face. 'And now it looks as though you are going to swoop down and kidnap him from us!'

There was no doubt about it, this was an opportunity any young sportsman would have grabbed at. But Gary was different. He was humble. Yes, he had the confidence and some bravado but there was a hesitancy in his manner that worried and delighted Zee in equal measures.

A deal was signed. Gary's club did very well out of it. Gary was signed up and joined the stable of Olympus. Zee added a clause that Gary should live with his family; he felt a solid home life would help add balance to the young man's life. The whole team at Olympus was overjoyed that Gary was joining them. They had recognised the excitement in Zee's demeanour around Gary and any positive move for Olympus was a positive gain for all of them. Hera was happy too. She was as important in Gary's future as everyone else. An exciting future was mapped out both for Gary and for Zee.

Over the years that followed, the training, the exposure, the careful managing and the support of Zee and Hera worked wonders. Gary did truly have magnificent all-round football skills and was courted by managers from around Europe. He played for several top teams from the very beginning, huge amounts being offered as transfer fees. His profile was high on the field and Zee, and, to some extent, Hera, made sure he cultivated a high profile off the field too. In his early twenties Gary developed into a strikingly handsome man and was hardly ever out of the newspapers and magazines. His future was guaranteed on the field for many years to come and on the back of this, modelling and product endorsement would ensure a life after football.

Zee and Gary became very close during these years. Gary had never had a father figure he could look up to and Zee not only found in Gary a son he had never had, but also someone to pass on his experience and values to, a new ... him.

Zee was obsessed by the young man, and Gary hung on his every word. Hera watched on.

Obviously, Gary spent much time away from the Idas' home as he played in teams around Europe, but the management team and agents kept a close eye on him. They made sure his public profile was high and that reports were sent back to London on a regular basis. Gary had many a beautiful young goddess on his arm at many an occasion and there was much gossip around whom he might settle down with.

But what only Zee and Hera knew, and what was desperately kept from the media and the public, was that Gary was gay. The homelife that Zee and Hera had provided for Gary had given him the grounding and the confidence to be himself when with them. They had become not only his mentors and managers, but the parents he never really had. They realised, above everything, that for Gary to be successful and to not crash and burn with the strain, he needed people he could be honest with, to be able to talk to.

But Zee and Hera worried for Gary. What personal happiness did the future hold for him?

Would he remain, trapped in this awful personal hell to protect his professional career, or would he, at some time, feel the need to be free of this artificial constraint and strain? The next few years would be glorious and yet difficult. Would he become the immortal star, remembered not only for his skill on the field but also, his public bravery?

At the end of the second decade of the twenty-first century, there are hardly any playing professional male footballers who have felt safe enough to publicly state that they are homosexual. A shocking fact. How many Garys are out there?

It should be noted that women's football is far more embracing and has many openly lesbian footballers.

A heartfelt tribute should also be paid to Justin Fashanu, who came out in 1990. It did not go well for his career and tragically he took his own life eight years later in 1998.

10

GOOD KING RICHARD

Richard I is an icon for some gay men. The story that has grown up around him presents the image of a handsome, dashing man, gallivanting around Europe on his steed. But he had a secret, which I reveal in this story. I have had a little bit of fun with history.

Ah, the Lady Melusine. The oldest of three daughters, she had been cursed by her mother for taking vengeful actions against her father (a story for another time). And her curse? Once a week she would turn into a fish-like creature with a scaly tail.

And so now she sat alone, by the bank of her beloved river, and thought of the life that could have been. She still lived well, in a handsome house with her trusted servants, but she stayed well away from polite society, choosing instead a bucolic life in her valley.

But the fame of her beauty spread far and wide. Sitting on the bank of the river, combing her hair, or staring into the distance in deep contemplation, she made a pretty picture. Passers-by spread these images, tempting young noblemen to travel to meet her, to try to win her heart. She would have none of it. It was not just the fear of them discovering her curse; no, it was the young men themselves she took a dislike to. They were inflated with the thrill of the hunt, full of self-importance, and the surety that they were the one that she would choose. Of course, she never did. Their coarse words offended her, the offers they tempted her with were laughable, and she sent them away coldly, with no hope of a second chance.

But one day something unusual happened. While she was sitting by the river reading, a young man came by on a beautiful horse. He dismounted and quietly led his horse down to the cool flowing water. He greeted her pleasantly and then sat down to watch his horse drink. And so began the simplest of conversations. He was the Duke of Aquitaine and happened to be staying in the area. He knew nothing of her or her reputation and seemed genuinely interested in the parts of her story she chose to tell him. They laughed, they talked, and sometimes they sat in comfortable silence, and when he stood to leave, she felt sad he was going.

'I hope that I might see you again soon,' one thought and the other said.

Over the next few days and weeks, they often chanced upon each other in different parts of the valley. They became friends and then one day came the request that she had often brushed off with a callous laugh: 'Will you do me the honour of marrying me?'

Her hesitancy caused him no concern; he merely sat and waited for her to gather her thoughts. Though she agreed, she did share with him a doubt she had: it was not about him but herself. She had lived for so long alone in this valley, away from the bustle of castle life, and she worried that she would find the constant demands on her hard. 'I feel that I would need space, time to call my own. Does that worry you?'

'On the contrary,' he said. 'This life you have led has made you the person you are.'

And so, a prenuptial agreement was decided upon. She would become his wife, his duchess, and she would have one day a week alone in her own apartments.

The rest of the story was a fairy tale. They did indeed marry. The wedding was a beautiful celebration of their love. Their life together proved to be everything each of them had hoped for. They had twelve children and all of them were loved dearly. There was much laughter in the castle and life was good. Melusine took her weekly away day as agreed and always came back refreshed and, in the duke's eyes, even more beautiful. Life was indeed good. But …

One day, the duke's brother came visiting. The duke provided a sumptuous meal and the two of them sat down together to catch up on each other's news. 'Will your wife be joining us?' asked the duke's brother.

The duke explained the weekly arrangement. No, she would not be joining them.

The brother furrowed his brow. 'Your wife has a whole day a week alone in her apartments, and you do not visit her there or even know what she is doing?'

The duke explained that the arrangement worked for them, that it had done so since their marriage many years ago and it benefitted Melusine greatly. 'She always returns radiant.'

The duke's brother could not believe the foolishness of this arrangement. How could she be his wife and he not know everything that she did? A wife should be open with her husband in everything. Who knows what she could be doing or whom she could be meeting each week?

And, although this arrangement had worked perfectly well for many years, the duke suddenly became troubled and doubted his wife. He was so stirred by his younger brother's words that he immediately excused himself and hurried to his wife's apartments. His heart was pounding, not only by the thought of what he might discover but by how foolish he had been all these years.

He arrived at the apartments and looked around. His wife's women-in-waiting looked worried and confused, which only added to his suspicions. They indicated that she was in her closet, taking a bath.

The duke headed for the door, but sense prevailed and instead of throwing back the door, he peered through a knothole instead. His shoulders relaxed as he saw the beautiful scene: his darling wife of so many years, relaxing in a large tub of water.

He was just about to creep away before his wife became aware of his doubts, when she turned in the water and a huge, scaly fish-tail flopped over the side of the tub! He was so shocked that he gasped loudly and in the midst of a flurry of splashing water, the sound of a door being thrown back and loud apologies being shouted, she was gone.

It was not just that he now knew of her curse, it was also the lack of trust after so many years, and in her desperation, she managed to make her way from the bath to the castle window and throw herself into the river that flowed below. He saw her tail splash in the water before it disappeared beneath the flowing current, never to be seen again.

The duke was distraught, angry with his brother, but also with himself. For the first time in his marriage, he had not thought first about his wife's feelings. Now he had to bear the consequences.

It is said that he mourned his loss, but he loved his children and he promised his departed wife that he would care for and cherish them. They all grew up to be fine young adults. Several of them married into royal families and over the years, many famous and powerful royal lineages proudly included Melusine and the Duke of Aquitaine in their family trees.

In the twelfth century, Henry II, the King of England – who in those times ruled not only England but also a large part of what we now call France – married Eleanor of Aquitaine. Initially it was a happy and successful marriage and Eleanor was delivered of four boys who survived infancy: young Henry, Richard, Geoffrey and John. A fifth son died very young.

But as Henry II grew older, his wife began to think of him as weak and openly encouraged her sons to rebel against their father in the hope that Henry the younger could become king, and the three other brothers powerful in their own right.

At one point, Eleanor defected to the court of the young French king, Phillip II, the sworn enemy of her husband. Her three elder boys joined her, while John, the youngest, stayed with his father. It was a stressful time for all concerned, but it seems that the three boys, now young men, relished the opportunities to rile their father even more by consorting with the enemy.

Richard was by all accounts a fine-looking young man. He was tall, over six feet, had a head of strawberry blond hair, and was a celebrated soldier. The young King Phillip was taken by the powerful yet charming character of his enemy's son, and soon a friendship blossomed between them. Richard loved the idea of his father receiving messages about his closeness to the young French king and, in truth, there were many accounts of their time together that would have angered and shocked Henry.

Courtiers and commentators of the time were well aware that the friendship had turned into something far more intimate. It was written that:

> Richard, [then] duke of Aquitaine, the son of the king of England, remained with Philip, the King of France, who so honoured him for so long that they ate every day at the same table and from the same dish, and at night their beds did not separate them. And the king of France loved him as his own soul; and they loved each other so much that the king of England was absolutely astonished at the passionate love between them and marvelled at it.

Time moved on and their relationship became stronger. Richard agreed to marry his lover's sister Alyce, but years passed and this never happened.

Their time together survived many battles between England and France, the death of Richard's older brother, young Henry, and finally the coronation of Richard as King of England after the death of his father. As king, Richard hardly visited England at all and concerned himself more with maintaining his French lands and his plans for crusades to the Holy Land, and his relationship with Phillip stayed strong. Until, somehow, it came to a mysterious and unchronicled end. Read on, dear reader, and I shall reveal all.

The two kings were powerful men, rulers of huge tracts of land, warriors who lived fast, hard lives and undoubtedly, their private time must have been important, maybe even precious to them. Meetings held at each other's various residencies would have had a political element but no doubt included some private time spent in each other's company.

One day, Phillip had something that he wanted to share with Richard, but he couldn't be found. Phillip knew straight away where he would be. Richard enjoyed time alone in his apartment.

The servants seemed flustered by his arrival and said that Richard was bathing. But the French king playfully motioned to them to be quiet and to get out. How delightful to creep up on his lover and catch him in the pleasures of bathing? He rested his long sword on the ground next to him as he placed his hands on the doorframe and leant in to spy on his lover through a knothole in the door. And there he was, luxuriating in the bath, his handsome torso dripping with water.

The Duke of Aquitaine, now King Richard I, was all he desired in a man and he delighted in this scene. Richard leant back against the tub rest and stretched his arms out sideways to ease the strain of his magnificent shoulder and arm muscles. As he changed position, a huge fish-tail slapped over the side of the tub, sending water everywhere!

Phillip jumped back from the door, covering his mouth in

horror and disgust. He forced himself to take another look, to check if what he had seen was a mistake, but to his horror, no ... Perhaps all the rumours of the English being devils or monsters were true, and he had only just discovered it after all these years.

He grabbed his sword, turned quickly from the scene and hurried down the castle passageways, angry and confused. He would never return to Richard's side again.

Richard led a successful, if restless, life, fighting in battles throughout Europe and the Middle East. He did marry, to Berengaria of Navarre, with much pomp and circumstance, but it was a political union, and even though she accompanied him on one crusade, they returned separately, and he never saw her again. He died in 1199 without a legitimate heir. He ended his last earthly day in the arms of his mother.

11

CONVERSATION

Music plays a great part in my life and 'Conversation' is one of my favourite songs by the great Joni Mitchell. Here is a story around the words of that song, as if it were written for a man's voice.

I had travelled round most of Europe that summer – well, some of it – a twenty-year-old and his guitar, busking to make a living. My parents and friends had been horrified when I announced how I was going to spend the holidays but then, as I said (or was it shouted?): 'It's my life and I am going to live it how I think best.'

I had worked really hard at uni for the past two years and the final year was looming darkly. I just had to have a break, a complete break and … I hate to use this term, but I had to sort my head out.

And so I had started in Germany – but only because I had a bit of schoolboy German – then swiftly moved on to Switzerland and swiftly on again (it was far too expensive) to Northern Italy and then the south of France. I had some savings from a small inheritance. I hitched lifts, sometimes worked in bars and cafés, and busked. I stayed in holiday places, found a busy square, plaza, piazza, and played my guitar and sang. I had often played gigs at university and so was quite happy to perform, but I must admit I was a bit staggered at how much I actually made. I wasn't having to dig into my inheritance all that much. Some places it was unofficial, others you had to have signed permission from the town hall, or you got moved on. Some towns encouraged my busking – I think it gave these chic places atmosphere – restaurants welcomed me and it was quite a buzz to draw a crowd. I even had a few references from some towns, which helped out at the next place of call. Accommodation varied from place to place.

So here I was now in Nice. Very nice. I had heard that official permission was needed, so off I went to the town hall and, armed with my 'references', was accepted as an official busker and was even given a map of places I could call my own.

I found some comfortable cheap digs down a back street and that first night just walked around the streets getting a feel for the place.

The next week or so was a breeze. The weather was so pleasant, the holidaymakers and tourists generous. The locals began to acknowledge me too.

One square in particular was my favourite. In the evening it was cool and shady and was circled by cafés and bars. By the middle of the evening there was an exhilarating buzz to the place, and by the end of the night it became a calm, upmarket eating and drinking place for the locals. It was not just about the cash; I actually enjoyed busking there. In between sets I would sit at a café with a coffee and watch the world go by. Some of the locals had got to know my name and would sometimes shout to me or even pay my bill.

I had plenty of space to get my head together. I'd had a lot of time to think, think about me, not my career or my studies or my family and friends, just me. I had come to a decision. And it was that night, quite by chance, perhaps now my mind was open, that I first saw him.

I was singing some quiet, mellow songs when I looked up and caught sight of him and he of me. Some of my songs had lyrics about catching somebody's eye across a room or a party but they had just been lyrics ... until now. Our eyes truly met across the square. He nodded and smiled and I flashed him a grin while still trying to keep the singing and playing going. He turned back to his friends, which gave me the chance to watch him. He was probably in his late twenties – handsome, it goes without saying. I couldn't quite make out what nationality he was. He was about my height but with dark wavy hair and eyes like deep pools that I could dive right into. He was obviously popular with his friends and had the most beautiful laugh that made my heart beat faster!

I finished my songs, there was applause from the cafés, and I did my usual tour of the tables to get my 'wages'. It was a good night. When I reached the young man's table, all were generous but there was an 'Ooooh' when he dug deep into his pocket and placed the bank note in my hat. We smiled at each other when I said thank you, and I could feel his friends looking at us. But then there was a stir of chairs as he and his friends suddenly stood and turned. A beautiful blonde woman had swept onto the café terrace. The others parted to let her join them and the young man kissed her on the cheek before offering her his chair. I watched and just smiled and went on with my collection. She sat with her arm around his neck but talking to their friends, and suddenly she was the centre of attention. Over her shoulder she said something to the young man and his smile faded.

That night in my room I lay awake for some time. There was a large Mediterranean moon and a welcome breeze blew the curtains inwards. As I lay there I knew that my long conversations with myself over the last few months had all been worthwhile. That smile kept coming back to me and that laugh rang in my ears like sweet bells. But I also realised I still had a lot to learn ... I had to perfect my radar – or was it 'gaydar'?

The following day, as I walked through the streets, there were lots of young men around, young men with nice smiles, but none compared with that smile last night. How could I have got it so wrong?

At lunchtime I bought some bread, cheese, tomato and a soda, and sat on the grass under a tree. I was miles away, tearing into the bread when I felt a strong hand on my shoulder. It was him.

'Hey, man.' An English accent. 'Can I share your feast?' Without waiting for my answer, he sat on the grass next to me and put out his hand. 'Adam,' he said.

How apt, I thought. The name of the first man.

'John,' I said as I took the strong hand in my grip.

The conversation was pretty ordinary, a sketchy outline of each other's life, but I felt comfortable in his company and he seemed at ease with me, but there was a definite sadness behind those dark eyes. We shared the food and drink and when we had consumed most of it, he suddenly realised what was happening ...

'Hey, I've eaten nearly all your food ... What am I thinking? Sorry, John. Listen, let me buy you a meal sometime.'

To say my heart skipped a beat is an understated cliché, but I gathered myself and said, 'Well, that's okay, don't worry. I usually come down here about this time every day. Your shout next time?'

'You're on. See you here tomorrow. Must fly now. Believe it or not, I do have work to get to.'

And off he went.

And so that's how our friendship began. Sharing a picnic lunch every now and again. I knew I had to be careful of my feelings, but it became easier as he began to tell me more about his life ... and his girlfriend.

He did seem to live a charmed life, but I couldn't help still feeling that there was something wrong, something troubling him, though he never gave any indication of it.

I saw him most evenings at the café bar, that handsome, happy guy with the beautiful eyes, enjoying life with his friends. But whenever his beautiful blonde girlfriend appeared – and she always arrived later than him – the atmosphere changed. He changed. His smile faded. He faded.

I still sang my songs, collected my wages and drank coffee at the other side of the square, but Adam never openly acknowledged our friendship. He and his friends were always pleased to see me, shouted requests and were very generous, but that was it. And when the blonde arrived, she never acknowledged me at all, never even looked at me ... But then again, she never really looked at Adam either. He always kissed her when she arrived, but then so did all their other friends. She always took the seat he offered her but never included him in her conversations, never even smiled at him – just that arm around his neck as though she wanted everyone to know that she possessed him; that he was hers.

We did manage to talk about it a little. Sometimes now he would come back to my bedsit and we would sit on the little balcony and drink wine and eat fruit and cheese. It was a bit of a shabby place and he was obviously used to so much better, but he seemed to feel at ease here and he began to open up. And I discovered the sadness.

He was trapped. Trapped by life here. Trapped by the blonde beauty. They had been together quite a while. She was rich, and although he had a good job, spoke fluent French and had many friends, he said that he never felt important in her life; he had become just another of her possessions. Although quite a catch himself, he was not vain and was certainly not over-confident, he just couldn't see any way forward. And yet he couldn't see how he could leave her. I suppose he was saying that he loved her.

I had to be careful now. There was so much I could tell him, advice I could give, opinions ... but I didn't know the full story and I had to keep my feelings for him out of the picture. I just let him talk, tried to make him laugh and sang him songs that he liked, but I wished I could dive in those deep pools. I had freed up my mind over the last few months. I wished I could free him.

One day he asked me if I knew a certain song. I had heard it, but a long time ago. I wasn't sure of the words, or even the tune. It was obviously a great favourite of his because although in the past he had never shown any inclination to join in with my singing, apart from humming or tapping his knee, he now joined in with gusto to teach me the words and the tune. His voice did not match his looks or personality, and we laughed so much trying to put the song together that a neighbour shouted about siesta time and could we keep it down?

Sniggering and trying to cover up our laughs, we shot into the room. He fell on the bed in fits of giggles and for the first time I saw him released from that sadness. His beauty absolutely shone through.

After a few minutes he pulled himself together and wiped his eyes, but then suddenly realised the time. 'Hey, work calls! Must fly. I've not enjoyed myself so much for a long time. I hope I can get some work done! See ya later, fella.'

And, with that, he whisked out of the room but left his presence.

I picked up my guitar and began to sing the song ... and found that, although we had been messing about and laughing, I had actually picked up the tune and was able to scribble down the words. I worked on it all afternoon. If it meant so much to him, it meant a lot to me.

That night, when the tourists had gone and the locals inhabited the bars, I watched the usual gang of Adam's friends arrive and then Adam himself. Was I imagining it? Did he look different? The blonde girl arrived, and the usual kissing, greeting and chair ritual took place. But Adam seemed much lighter, his face was alive, and the blonde girl did look at him occasionally. I could see him joining in the conversation more, and making their friends laugh.

I sang for my supper as I usually did, had requests shouted to me and had encouraging nods from the bar owners and drinks sent over.

And then when the evening settled into that mellow time of night, I began to sing that song. I felt comfortable with it; from the beginning it flowed well and I was interested to note that the group of friends went quieter. They were looking at the blonde, who now was looking down at the floor. Adam leant forward and whispered in her ear. There was a several-second pause and then ... she threw back her head and let out a truly happy laugh. She stood up and turned to Adam and threw her arms around him. The whole group of friends laughed and cheered and almost clapped. The couple hugged each other, turned to their friends and began to say their goodnights. Hand in hand they turned and almost ran round the corner.

I carried on with the song as best as I could; emotion is always a good tool for performers. When I finished, the applause was more generous than usual and the collection very profitable. The atmosphere at Adam's table was light and cheerful.

I could have asked why the song had had such an effect, but I didn't think I could cope with the answer.

As usual, I wiped my guitar before I put it back in its case. I looked around at this near perfect piece of heaven where I had enjoyed many an evening doing what I enjoyed most. I gulped down the last of my coffee.

It was time to go home.

12

THE SELKIE

A selkie is a marvellous creature that lives most of its life as a seal, but is able to come ashore and step out of its sealskin and take on the form of a human being. It returns to its true home, the sea, by stepping back into its skin again.

The selkie is a useful metaphor for many situations but is particularly appropriate for some in the LGBTQ+ community. We all sometimes have two or more personas, choosing the one that makes us feel safe, comfortable or appropriate at a given time.

When I first came to terms with my sexuality at forty-six, I suddenly found myself single and on the dating scene. I felt I needed to take on a new skin, or step out of my regular one, to 'fit in' with my new life. So, I joined a gym.

On my first visit I was given a tour of the equipment and asked to fill in a form. The gym was in West Yorkshire and the man helping me was young enough to be my son. Early on he asked me if I had any support at home in my new fitness routine and I told him I was just out of a marriage, so, no. He showed me around and several times we stopped at large rooms where classes were held.

'If you're hoping to meet the woman of your dreams, this is a good class to enrol in. There are lots of single women here.'

He was sweet and trying to be so positive! But after the third time I felt I had to put him straight: it was the man of my dreams I was looking to meet.

He almost stepped back in surprise. 'Well, I would have never guessed that, you're so butch. And I know,' with a knowing nod of his head, 'I've been to London!'

Bless him.

I only managed a few sessions at the gym before I damaged my knee so I made the decision to be happy in my own skin.

Sitting on a rock at the edge of her cove, Anna couldn't imagine how life could get any better. Yet living this life was a double-edged blessing.

She had been an only child. Hers had been liberal parents, raising Anna to be strong-minded and very much her own person. They had owned a cottage high on the cliffs and farmed the surrounding land organically, something that was unusual in the seventies and eighties. Anna had attended a local school and then her parents had funded her through art college, which must have been quite a strain on their finances. She was successful with her studies and the future looked bright, but she soon found that trying to make a living in the commercial art world was not easy. She tried many avenues, but it literally didn't pay, and she had to take up work temping.

And then, one day, her whole world changed. Her mother and father were killed in a road accident.

The house and farmlands were left to her. She moved back to the house and sold off the land. With a healthy bank balance, somewhere to live, and a lifestyle that was perfect for painting, she could now live the life she had always dreamed of. But what a price she had paid.

She was determined to, at the very least, make her parents proud of her.

So she spent many hours on the rocks in the little cove that was at the bottom of a flight of steps from the house. It was a truly beautiful place: a small inlet protected from the worst of the elements with a slim strip of shingle beach, and pools of every hue, embraced by two arms of rock that went out into the ocean. The air was filled with gulls and the rocks were covered in many types of seaweed. Shoreline plants sprouted from the bottom of the cliffs and there were seals – oh, the seals – bobbing about in the rise and fall, watching her, following her with those delicious eyes. She loved observing them swim but it was when they pulled themselves out onto the rocks in the middle of the cove that her heart beat quickly at how beautiful they were. She loved to sketch them lying in twos and threes, so close to each other, with their flippers gently laid across their friends like protective arms. She spent so much time there that they began to approach her more closely but, with the slightest movement – the turning of her sketchbook pages, or reaching for her paints – they would plunge into the depths. There was one, braver than the rest, who sometimes stayed longer. She had a stripe of silver grey amongst the mottled browns on her head.

'Hello there, beautiful,' Anna would call. 'How are we today, beautiful – Bella – Belle?'

Her artwork was progressing. She was beginning to get a feel for the colours and the lines and the reflections of this precious place. Her sketches were very detailed. Close drawings and little watercolour paintings of a certain rock formation, a clump of seaweed, shells, pebbles, clouds, gulls and Belle. When she returned to the cottage, she reworked the pieces sitting at the large table she had placed in the main window. Her materials and pictures were scattered in an untidy, reasoned way around her. But she had not yet grasped where to progress with them. What was the bigger picture?

There was one concern in her life, one she was not sure how to deal with. A young lad from the nearest town had begun to cause trouble. It was quite a bike ride and an even longer walk for him but just occasionally he would appear on the cliff top, or halfway down the steps; sometimes along the bay. He enjoyed disturbing her peace. Nothing serious, but it troubled her. He shouted abuse, horrible comments. They sounded too adult for him, so she guessed he was getting this from grown-ups at home or older teenagers. Words that cut her to the very bone: 'Hey, girlie. You're looking very queer today! Dyke!'

They were only words and he did run off when she stood up. But now she made sure that her doors and windows were locked before she came down to the cove, something her family had never had to do before. He hadn't been around for some time, thank goodness.

One summer evening, she went down to the cove to catch the dimming light on the water and the rocks. She sat there alone for several hours before she noticed how late it was. She could lose hours when she was working. It was quite dark now, with just the light of a part moon and attending stars shimmering on the water. It was such a still evening, no breeze. The familiar sounds of the cove resonated louder than usual. The swishing of the tide on the shingle, the loud plops of the odd wave catching an unusual rock formation. And as she sat silently, taking it all in, she was suddenly aware of the seals bobbing around. They had not noticed her and as she sat there in the darkness, quietly, there was a thrill inside her as she watched them swim around together, playing, like a family. Like a family? In that second, she realised how lonely she had become.

The seals swam on together and disappeared round a large outcrop of rock and all was quiet again. She sat there thinking and then she heard voices, laughter, splashing, running on the shingle?

She stood up to listen more closely but even in that stillness, she could not make out where the noise was coming from or even if it was human.

But then she heard a voice she definitely knew. 'Hey girlie, queer to see you out at night. Seals your only friends? Well, I'll show them!'

Suddenly she began to hear loud splashes in the water around her and on the rocks. He had begun pelting her with stones, emboldened by the darkness. His words, which should not have hurt her, were made more painful by 'sticks and stones'. But this time, she was not worried about herself. It was the seals she was concerned about. If they had beached on the shingle at the other side of the rocks and were making the noises she had heard earlier, then he could hurt them.

'Stop it!' she shouted, running towards the rocks. 'Stop, you wicked little bastard!'

It worked. The 'wicked little bastard' turned and made for the steps in a hurry.

Anna scrambled over the rocks in the darkness. She saw movement, scurrying, splashing, slithering, as the seals somehow made it back into the water. It was a strange sight! She watched them swim out and disappear beneath the waves and sighed with relief.

Then she noticed a shape – a woman – sitting on the rocks. Anna's mind worked at twice the speed as she tried to make sense of this. Had this all been a horrible coincidence? The seals, the awful boy throwing rocks, the sound of laughter and a woman out walking or maybe even swimming? Had she been hurt by the rocks in all the commotion?

'Hello, are you OK?' Anna ventured as she approached the figure. 'Do you need any help?'

Slowly, the woman turned her head towards Anna. Her long, grey-streaked brown hair was wet and plastered to her naked shoulders. She had some sort of sarong wrapped around her. She stood and turned to Anna but swayed a little, as though she might faint. Anna dashed forward and caught her.

'I live just at the top of those steps,' she said. 'It's a bit of a climb but I can help you. Come and have a sit down, a cuppa. I can call the police if you want me to?'

In her head, Anna heard, 'Thank you, you are very kind.'

She took the weight of the woman and they slowly made their way across the rocks to the bottom of the steps. The woman stopped when she saw the rise of the steps and looked back over her shoulders towards the sea.

'Don't worry, we can take our time,' Anna said.

Slowly, the two climbed the steep mountain.

Anna sat her on a bench on the veranda, while she fumbled for the key. When she turned back to the woman she was looking up at Anna with soulful brown eyes. Anna noticed that she was naked apart from the animal-print sarong.

'Come on in. Let's get you comfortable and dry. I'll make you a cuppa. Do you drink tea?'

She sat the woman next to the fire and returned with a large towel, which she exchanged for the sarong. It was heavy and damp and felt like an animal skin.

'Here, let me help you.' She wrapped the towel around the woman and then threw some wood on the fire to stoke it up.

'There, that's much better isn't it? Can I get you anything else? What's your name, by the way?'

'Belle,' Anna heard in her head.

Had you been able to look in through the window over the next hour or so, you would have seen Anna, scuttling about the room, in and out of the door into other rooms, fetching a dressing gown, a blanket, holding up the phone to Belle, handing her a cuppa, all the time talking away to her visitor in an animated way. You would not have seen Belle replying or talking at all, yet Anna could hear all the replies to her questions.

No, Belle didn't need anyone calling. She would be fine just sitting here for a while. Yes, she had been swimming in the cove. No, she had not been hit by a rock. And so on.

At last Anna asked if she would like to stay at the cottage for the night. 'We can get you home tomorrow when you've rested.'

Anna helped Belle to her feet and showed her into her bedroom. She pulled back the covers and Belle dropped her gown on the floor and lay down.

'I'll just be next door if you need me. Call if you need anything.'

'Please, stay with me,' Anna heard.

Belle pulled back the covers. Anna stared at her, took off her boots and socks and jeans, and wearing her pants and tee-shirt, she gingerly lay down beside Belle. She lay there for a few minutes and then turned on her side, her back to Belle. Belle moved a little closer and a protective arm came across Anna. They slept.

And so began their life together. Anna was amazed at how quickly the two of them struck up such a close friendship, as though they had known each other much longer.

Belle spent all her time in the house, almost as if it were a sanctuary. She would look out of the large windows towards the sea, but she never ventured through the door and seemed quite content to spend her time looking at Anna's possessions, sitting in the chair, lying on the bed and answering all of Anna's questions as best she could. She loved to watch Anna work. She would stand behind her, sometimes with her hands on Anna's shoulders, and watch her paint.

Anna began to paint as she had never done before. Now Belle was around, the many detailed drawings and little paintings were coming together to create exciting seascape vistas and underwater scenes. Anna was excited to see her creations forming and she worked long hours, always with Belle watching.

Anna sometimes had to go out, to shop or even go down to the cove to collect more visual ideas, but Belle was quite content to stay behind.

When Anna came home, she was pleased to see that Belle was making herself useful, tidying the house, arranging things. Her boxes of shells and pebbles had been raided by Belle and some now sat in arrangements on shelves, on the floor and on the porch. Ah, Belle obviously ventured out when Anna wasn't there. Dresses and scarves from Anna's wardrobe were neatly laid out on the bed in the spare room and she had even laid the animal skin sarong over the bottom of the bed. Anna realised that the skin was important to Belle as it was the only reminder of her former life. It was almost her comfort blanket and Anna watched her some nights as she slept next to her, so beautiful, so peaceful, but with her fingers wound in the edges of the sarong.

Life carried on. Perfectly. Happiness ruled. Even the lad from town was not seen again.

During the hot summer, Anna wanted Belle to come down to the cove for a swim. Belle refused, although she did venture on to the veranda where it was cooler. Anna created a day bed for her so she could lie in the breeze and bask.

One day, while Belle was asleep on the veranda, Anna sorted some summer clothes for them both. She piled them on to a chair, went across to the bed, took the animal skin from the bed and folded it and put it in a drawer. It was too hot at night to have on the bed anyway. And then she laid out all the summer clothes on the bed for Belle to see when she woke up.

When Belle came into the bedroom, Anna proudly indicated the bed with a flourish of her arms and a dramatic, 'Ta dah!'

She didn't get the reaction she expected. Belle flew into a blind panic, scrabbling through the clothes, flinging them everywhere.

'Where is it?' Anna heard Belle scream.

She ran to the drawers, wrenched one open and handed Belle the sarong. Belle grabbed it and fell to the floor, clasping it to her face, crying uncontrollable sobs and animal howls.

'Oh, I'm so sorry, my darling, I didn't mean to upset you, but it was safe in the drawer. I would never throw it away. It's yours, it's part of you, part of your other life!'

Belle looked up at Anna. 'I'm sorry.'

Anna continued her work, watched over by Belle. She had noticed that Belle had begun to carry the sarong with her everywhere. But that was all right if it gave her comfort. And Anna's work progressed. Not only were the paintings filled with expression, they began to take on an otherworldliness. Ideas began to form in Anna's head about how she could gather them in a collection around a story. A picture book for adults! And the images grew, including Anna, Belle and the seals.

One afternoon, she arrived back at the house after a particularly long shopping trip. She sometimes tricked Belle into venturing further from the house by shouting for help to carry the shopping from the car. Belle had not been too keen to begin with, but could see it was not fair to leave the heavy carrying to Anna. Anna was pleased to see Belle out in the fresh air and the breeze blowing in her hair; the smell of the sea in her nostrils seemed to invigorate her.

'I'm back!' shouted Anna. 'Belle, can you come and help me please?'

But Belle did not appear.

'I bet she's asleep.' Anna grabbed several bags and staggered into the house, dumping them noisily on the table. 'Come on, sleepy head, earn your keep!'

But there was no sign of Belle stirring.

'Belle? Are you okay, honey?'

Anna looked around the empty house with increasing panic. Belle was nowhere to be found. She ran to the door but Belle was not in the garden either. She looked across to the cliff edge, to the gate that led the way to the steps to the cove.

'Surely not?'

Anna ran across the clifftop grass and through the gate. She began to scoot down the steps and halfway down, looked up and saw Belle on the rocks by the edge of the sea.

'Belle?' she shouted.

Belle obviously heard her, because she turned her head towards her, but instead of waving back, she turned to the sea. Anna ran down the steps, and as she reached the shingle, she looked up to see Belle beginning to take her clothes off. She scrambled across the rocks as fast as she could, realising that something was very wrong.

'Belle, wait, please!'

She noticed the seals bobbing about in the water and saw the now naked Belle begin to wrap that wretched sarong around her. Belle looked at Anna but then again at the sea and the seals. Anna saw her sway and then tumble towards the water and as she tumbled, Belle seemed to twist and dive. She disappeared beneath the water.

Anna could just see the head and outline of a seal, swimming toward the group further out. When she reached them, they all upended, tails in the air, and sank out of sight.

Anna stood there transfixed, her hands tightly over her mouth, and when she removed them, she heard herself wailing loudly, animal howls, as she fell to the rocks.

Anna worked at her art table, occasionally glancing out at the seascape that so inspired her to create. Everything was falling into place now and page after page of her pictorial book was completed with the addition of a simple storyline. She smiled as she thought of how proud her parents would be. A book that told of her story by the sea. The waves, the sound of the gulls, the rocks and pebbles, plants and seaweeds, the wonderful seals and of course Belle, the beautiful woman creature who had come into her life and changed it forever. The title of the book summed everything up for her: *Could Life Get Any Better?*

How could it? She now had a career, a passion, a life, and as she worked at that passion, she knew she would always have Belle standing behind her, with her hands resting gently on her shoulders, willing her to create more and more.

13

THE ARCHITECT

This is a story told to me by a friend many years ago. He gifted it to me at the time and told me to use it as I please. It never ceases to make me shudder when I read it through. Stories work best when they are shared and reworked.

John had worked at the architects' practice for only a couple of years, but he had proved himself again and again as an up-and-coming force. Many of his colleagues tipped that he would soon be asked to join the practice as a partner.

His whole life seemed to revolve around his work – or so his colleagues presumed. He was always early at work and the last to leave. He took work home with him and never talked about his home life at all. To his colleagues, he was a closed book.

And why was this? Well, it was simply that John was a private man.

His life did revolve around his work and his love of architecture, and he liked some of his workmates, but just because he worked with them, it didn't mean he wanted to socialise with them. In whatever free time he may have had, he liked to visit houses and buildings of interest, collect related books and acquire beautiful things.

He lived on his own in an apartment down by the river. It was a light and airy warehouse conversion and John had furnished it beautifully. It featured sleek lines and pale colours with a touch of an accent colour here and there. Design was important to him. He felt comfortable in his own space and arranged and maintained it immaculately.

On the walls were framed prints and originals of architectural plans, historical lithographs and photographs. And he had a treasured collection of miniature wooden houses. I say a collection; there were five or six, sourced keenly in the antique fairs and shops of southern England. The miniature models were made by master builders to entice the rich, as furniture makers of the Georgian and early Victorian periods had made exquisite samples of their furniture, in order to show prospective customers their designs and skills.

These early pieces were difficult to find, and John had persuaded himself, wisely, to limit his purchases to unusual pieces, the holy grails. To him, the search was almost as pleasing as the ownership, and he was prepared to pay a fair amount for each one.

He had therefore been taken by surprise by his most recent purchase, which was neither created by a particularly noted craftsman nor in an unusual style. No, it was the fact that this one had a figure in one of the windows, something he had never seen before. He presumed that the craftsman had cleverly used the figure to give the model some sort of scale for the untrained eye. Fascinating!

The place where he had found it had been more of a junk shop than an antique emporium. It was priced so low that the owner could not have realised its worth and when John had furrowed his brow (always a good technique to use when buying), the owner immediately halved the asking price.

Now it stood in the centre of John's hall table, taking pride of place.

Work became increasingly demanding as John was given more and more responsibilities and high-end contracts to work on. He rose to the occasion, meeting and negotiating with important clients, dealing in enormous budgets and fulfilling tight deadlines. This was what he had studied for all those years, what he had given his whole being to. Success.

The stress was strangely gratifying. It focused his mind and kept him on task, though it was beginning to affect his life. Meals were eaten on the hoof, indigestion ruled, and sleep patterns altered. John had always been a good sleeper and risen early, but lately he had been troubled by restless nights. At first, he thought nothing of it, but as time passed he became aware of fragments of dreams, strange images that popped up through the day while he was working. The main image involved a staircase which he felt compelled to climb to reach the very top. Nothing too odd about that. But as the nights progressed, John woke up increasingly distressed. Until one morning he realised why.

In his dream, the staircase was no ordinary flight of stairs. The first riser was around six feet high and each night he faced the torment of attempting to scale these huge stairs, each one needing immense strength and stamina. Some nights he managed to climb several, but then he would either wake up or fall for some reason and the utter disappointment at failing became unbearably distressing. He would wake up in a cold sweat, the bed covers thrown everywhere or tangled round his legs. Some mornings, he couldn't drag himself out of bed for some time, the tiredness and desperation feeling real.

He began to be late for work and mixed up clients and meeting times. Important clients started to complain to the senior partners about their concerns, but his bosses had faith in him. After all, he had never let them down before. This was obviously a blip, and so they let things pass.

But the dream seemed to occupy not only John's nights but also his working days. Colleagues noticed that he was looking unkempt, preoccupied and quieter than usual. Unkindly they felt he had brought this on himself: he had never been a team player and had stolen the limelight.

Meanwhile, in his dream, the increased effort that John put into climbing the stairs was beginning to pay off. Each night he got nearer and nearer the top but each night, as he failed to scale the very top step, the anguish got worse.

And then, one night, he made it.

He was too exhausted to be truly elated; he just needed to find out what was up here of so much importance before he woke up again.

A large landing spread before him, with many closed doors but then he noticed one that was open. He tentatively crept along the landing and peered through the gap the open door created. Inside was a simple room: a bedroom, with fine but basic furniture, but there, seated on a sofa facing the large bay window, was someone looking out. John quietly pushed the door open, and as he did so, the person turned around. It was a man. A man with sparkling eyes and a broad smile.

'Come on in, John, I've been waiting for you for such a long time.'

He indicated to John to come and sit down next to him. John walked across the room, looked at the man, then looked out at the view from the window.

'Isn't it beautiful, John? You can see everything so much more clearly from here.'

John looked out of the window and sank on to the sofa. It was truly astonishing how his mind cleared at the view.

He felt a hand on his thigh and couldn't help smiling.

No one really noticed that John didn't come into work the following morning. They just presumed it was a continuation of his current, erratic behaviour. But when he didn't turn up the next day either, his line manager phoned his mobile and landline, but both went to voicemail, and there was no reply to left messages. This was not usual behaviour: if John took time off for illness or a break away, he would phone in to explain.

At last one of the partners decided to call round, but there was no answer at the main door. Concern prompted a call to the concierge, who said that he had not seen John for some days.

John's sister was his next of kin. She came straight away and the two of them persuaded the concierge to allow them entrance to John's apartment.

John was found lying peacefully in his bed, pale and cold but with the faintest of smiles on his lips.

There was considerable shock and concern back at the office. Some felt guilt for not acting sooner, for not making an effort to know John better; others put it down to John being a loner, too private.

The partner who had discovered John took on the responsibility of helping his sister to sort out this dreadfully sad mess.

After it was all sorted, when the post-mortem had delivered its findings, and all the legal challenges had been straightened out, John could at last lie in peace.

At the final meeting between John's sister and the concerned partner at John's flat, she told him of her gratitude for all his help and concern. 'I'm sure John would have liked you to have something to remind you of him.'

At first the partner said there was no need, no need, but she insisted.

Standing in the hallway, he looked around and noticed the small wooden house. 'Very well, that's very kind of you. I will just take something small. Do you mind if I take this wooden house? I know John was passionate about architecture and this will be something appropriate to place in the office to remind us of him.'

She nodded tearfully and he picked it up.

'It's so unusual, too. I've come across these miniatures before, but I've never seen one with little figures in the window. It's charming: two little men sitting there enjoying the view!'

14

RED VELVET

Sometimes, two stories are perfect for weaving together to make into one story, a plait. Here are two such stories, two lives.

Thomas Clifton no doubt kissed his mother and father farewell as he set off that morning. There was nothing special about that day; just another schoolday for the thirteen-year-old.

His parents were proud of their son. He was slight of frame and had an angelic face. His studies were going well, and they were happy that their hard-earned wealth was providing him with a good education and a prosperous future. Hopefully he would be able to join one of the guilds with the qualifications he would achieve and – who knows? – create a fine career, get married and raise a family, own a fine house and be able to care for his parents when they became old.

And so off he set, his books and his meal wrapped in cloth, smart clothes, and a kiss on the forehead sending him on his way.

Chris sat at her desk in her room in the shared house. It was late at night. Blue smoke gently rose from a cigarette in an ashtray. The radio played quietly behind her and her desk lamp shone its sharp yellow beam down on to piles of notes and her keyboard. It was a small room, but it was hers. She liked working at this time of night, the quiet, the calm safety of the four walls hugging her, and she couldn't help but smile to herself. Yes, she deserved to smile, one of those deep, satisfied smiles that said, 'I did it, despite everything.'

She took a quick look around at her haven, took a deep breath, and dived into the world of higher education, this, her final essay.

Thomas walked down the streets towards his school, a grammar school funded by several of the local trade guilds. He was aware of how fortunate he was to be receiving such a prestigious education and he was going to prove to his parents just how much he valued their faith in him. Latin and Greek verbs filled his head as he carefully stepped around piles of human waste that had been thrown from the overhanging windows of shabby brown-and-white timbered houses that loomed over him as he made his way down the narrow, gloomy alleyways. He would

never get used to the smell and held his hand over his mouth and nose as he increased his pace. Even his young head knew the vast differences between these ordinary lives, going on around him, and the ones lived by the very rich, the nobility in their fine palaces. London was riddled with rat-infested alleyways but was also peppered with fine houses and palaces in garden spaces. He wondered if the queen threw the contents of her piss pot out of the window in the morning, or did she have someone to do it for her? His young thoughts were interrupted by the sound of cracking hooves on the filthy cobbles behind him. A man was riding towards him and Thomas stood back to let him pass.

Chris had grown up in a warm and caring family on a large, local authority housing estate. School was important, Mum was important, and time alone was important. From an early age Chris had felt different from friends in the playground and never invited them home to play in the back garden. Older siblings were kind, and tolerated, even encouraged, the odd quirks of the baby of the family. Only Dad had to be avoided. He was definitely the 'man of the house'. Mum was never allowed to earn her own money, and he expected the whole household to revolve around him. His food was always on the table when he got home from a hard day's work; the older children stayed out of his way and Chris hid behind Mum's skirts on many occasions. Dad liked order, conventionality and everything to be in its place. No one – no one – ever challenged his rules. And that was why Chris feared him.

Thomas stepped into the shadows of the overhanging roof to give way to the horseman but, to his surprise, the rider came to a halt and dismounted. Still hanging on to the reins, he walked towards Thomas, looked him closely in the face, grinned a toothy grin and grabbed him. Thomas screamed and dropped his books, but a hand roughly clapped over his face and he felt himself being manhandled up on to the horse. He was too stunned to fight back and before he knew it, the horse set off while he hung on for dear life. The horse jolted him about, and the man held tightly to a handful of his clothing and skin as Thomas passed out.

It didn't take drink or Chris being naughty to set Dad off in a rage; it was just the mere presence of his son. He sneered at the way Chris stayed near his mother, the way he liked to read books instead of playing out in the street with the other boys, and the way he didn't cry. Chris had worked out long ago that his father wanted to make him cry, so no tears ever rolled down his cheeks when his father was there, no matter what. And that infuriated his dad.

'Can't you just leave him alone, George? He's not doing anything to hurt you,' said his mother.

But once the rage started there was no stopping it. And when, one day, his father had caught him playing with his mother's shoes, the fog descended. Mother was able to snatch Chris before his father could grab him, and she took several punches that were aimed at him. But a mother's love knows no bounds and she fought like a wren against a huge tabby cat to protect her youngest. And she won. No one else heard what she said to her husband, apart from Chris, but from that day on, his dad never laid a hand upon him. True, he shouted or sneered dreadful insults at him but there was never physical violence dealt out. But you don't need blows to the stomach to hurt; a father's cursing hurts just as much.

When Thomas didn't arrive home that evening at the usual time, his parents were worried. Father decided to visit the school, even though it was probably empty by this time. He needed to do something. Mother told him the route she knew Thomas always took to school and then collapsed on a chair in tears. They both knew something was dreadfully wrong. Making his way along the same alleyways, hastily stepping over a pile of human waste, Thomas' father noticed the cloth that had been so carefully wrapped around Thomas' books, discarded and dirty on the ground. The books had vanished, no doubt stolen. And the food had been scattered by dogs or rats. But there was no sign of Thomas. His father stood in the street shouting Thomas' name before collapsing in distress. Neighbours from nearby houses came

to his aid, and an old man from the house opposite leaned out of his window and described what had happened.

Chris certainly gave his dad lots to sneer at during his growing years. Buoyed up by the knowledge that his father would no longer physically hurt him, he displayed, even flouted, all the traits of a troubled teenager. Chris was his own man too, but in his own way. He grew his hair, shaped and coloured it in endlessly changing styles, and applied make-up with more daring as he grew older and began to experiment.

He may not have been beaten up at home any more, but now at school and in clubs violence followed him. But strangely, he was happy, happier than he had ever been. There were times in his life, and new friends, that gave him strength, strength to grow and find out truly who he was.

But when his mother passed away suddenly, Chris knew it was time to move on too. Packing a bag and grabbing a few of his mother's clothes, he laughed in his father's face and left. As the door slammed behind him, he was unaware of his dad, sitting blankly in his chair, distraught and lost. But his father never came looking for him.

Thomas' father soon tracked down where his beloved son had been taken. The old man had said, 'A man from the theatre did haul, pull, drag and carry away your son.'

Thomas' father hurriedly made his way to the Blackfriars playhouse and demanded to see his son, but he was contemptuously dismissed and told that if his son did not learn his lines he would be whipped.

Thomas' father was a beaten man. It was well known that the queen, Good Queen Bess herself, had signed commissions giving 'playhouse owners the authority sufficient so to take any nobleman's son in the land'. How could he win against such heavy odds? Many theatres provided performances by children's troupes, often taking place in dimly lit theatres featuring predominantly male audiences, where the exploitation of these boys was often explicitly sexual.

As Thomas' father held his hands to his head, his only solace was that at least this theatre was not one of those. The Blackfriars playhouse presented popular plays where whole families visited. He had to tell his wife the dreadful truth and he hugged her through her screams and wailing. In time, Thomas was allowed home for visits.

The next ten years or so were hard for Chris as he stumbled from job to job, bedsitter to squat to sofa, and the people he met were diverse too. But he became a strong young man because of this and grabbed every experience he could and learned from it. He finally found himself a room in a comfortable shared house with the help of a charitable group and he now had time to plan his future.

As was normal, Thomas was put into lodgings while he initially learned his craft. It was usual for boy actors in reputable companies to be placed in the home of one of the established male actors and his family. The thought was that if the boy could spend as much time as possible with an actor, then he would become immersed in this full-time occupation. But also, he would spend time with the actor's wife so he could get to know what women were like, how they functioned and how they felt. If a teenage boy was to play the role of Cleopatra or Lady Macbeth or any one of the many leading women's roles, he had to have insight into how women lived, if they were to be portrayed faithfully on stage to a paying audience.

Chris decided to transition. She had always known that she was in the wrong body and had a good idea of who she wanted to be. Life had made her strong and had given her a maturity beyond her years. She could have got the money together somehow and taken herself off to Thailand and had everything done in one go, but no. Experience had shown her it was not that easy, and time was on her side. So, after registering at a clinic, she followed the suggested plan. She would spend the next two years living as a woman without any surgery. She kept the name Chris; she felt no need to change that. And she began to wear women's clothes all the time. She was in her late twenties by now, so no longer the delicate blossom she once had been. She still looked unmistakeably like a man and at first it proved difficult. In time, with the help of prescribed hormones, her body began to reshape, her voice softened and her hair changed. She relaxed into being a woman. And to help the time to speed by, she enrolled at university to study, gain qualifications and a future.

Thomas excelled in his new life. He took it as further learning and applied himself to his new craft as he had done with his Latin and Greek. He loved living with his adopted family, visiting his own parents from time to time, and of course performing. The roar of the audience on his first entry, the wails of grief when he played doomed heroines, the laughter and coarse jeers from the comedy audiences, thrilled him. He particularly enjoyed the plays where he, as a boy, was playing a young woman who dressed up as a boy, and, as in the part of Viola, then flirted with the leading man on behalf of his mistress. The comments and knowing laughter from the standing audience was priceless. And there were the costumes and wigs too. Thomas felt no shame in wearing these; they were an essential part of who he was now. He particularly loved a rich, ruby-red velvet dress that made an appearance in several plays. Only the most reputable theatre companies could afford costumes such as these.

Chris read through her final study. She had spent weeks researching and putting it together. The word count was fine, the references and credits were complete, and she was delighted with the form, especially the addition of the story of Thomas, which somehow raised what could have been a dry tome into something with life.

The boys who played female roles on the stage grew into men with the passage of time. But what happened to them when their voices deepened and they began to change physically? Many continued acting female roles. As they grew older, they played the older, more comic characters and they often lived 'female' lives. Others moved on to play the male roles and find fame and fortune that way, perhaps even in the future taking a young boy actor under their wing. Many became womanisers and others stable, family men. It is thought that their knowledge of women, gained through playing female roles, gifted them with the ability to truly satisfy women, to know what a woman wanted, either in the guise of womaniser or husband.

And as for Thomas? We do not know what happened to him, his story lost in time. Maybe he still acted and after performances, at the stage door, had many a dalliance with women from the adoring audience; possibly he settled down into family life. Or maybe, he carried on his female acting career, enjoying too much the fine, ruby-red, velvet dress and how it made him feel.

Chris smiled to herself. She carefully closed the manuscript of her bound essay and looked at the front page where her name proudly sat. And the title? 'Boy Players in the Elizabethan Theatre.'

The essay had to be handed in tomorrow. But now, it was time to treat herself. Her favourite ruby-red, velvet dress was hanging on the back of the door. It was time to party.

15

THE MISTLETOE BOUGH

This well-known story is disturbing in its original form. Hopefully my additions add a different twist.

Imagine, if you will, a small but perfectly formed castle, in middle England in the Middle Ages, a castle and its land owned by a well-loved and respected lord and lady.

The lord and lady had been blessed with one child, a boy called Gregory, whom they loved and nurtured. As the years passed he grew into a fine young man, educated and thoughtful.

When Gregory was sixteen, his parents decided that it was time he married and so began a search for the perfect young woman. She too needed to be educated, beautiful and dutiful, the ideal future lady of the castle.

And so servants, elders and priests were sent north, south, east and west to find this perfect young woman. After many months of searching, word came of a young woman, the daughter of a fine family from the kingdom of Northumbria. Messages were sent back and forth between the two sets of parents. At last it was decided: the family from the north would travel south, to the castle in the Midlands.

Before the journey, the lord and lady from the north shared their plans with their daughter Gwen. The daughter listened carefully and, being a dutiful young woman, agreed to the plan, even though it was rumoured among the servants at the castle that she already had a sweetheart – some even said a lover.

It was early December when the family from the north made the journey south with servants and soldiers. After several days of travelling, they arrived at the castle in the Midlands.

The two families met for the first time in the castle courtyard. When the two young people stepped forward to greet each other, it was obvious to everyone that they made a wonderful couple.

Gwen curtsied low, her eyes downward. Gregory also bowed low, gazing intently at her captivating face, but as he did so, he noticed a slightly older man standing close by her, a little too close. It was the family steward. As Gregory bowed, the two men caught each other's eye and exchanged a slight nod of recognition. You see, Gregory had heard the rumours too, from his faithful servants!

But any worries Gregory had seemed to be unfounded. The steward proved to be an excellent servant to the family and was appointed chaperone to the young couple. Time was given for Gregory and Gwen to get to know each other and the steward was always to hand. He was a man of the world, thoughtful as to the situation, and realised that the couple also needed some private time together. He therefore, occasionally, withdrew a discreet distance to give the young couple time alone, but Gregory noticed that, even from a distance, the steward never took his eyes off him. Gregory was impressed and would smile at the steward in appreciation of his concern for Gwen's care and that he took his duties as chaperone seriously.

The time spent alone together, talking, laughing and planning, meant that the young couple fell quickly in love. Gregory and Gwen, although both so young, made a wonderful couple. Their parents were delighted that their arrangement was working, and it was decided that the marriage should take place within the week. The whole castle became as busy as a beehive with preparations and, yet again, the steward stepped up to the mark, helping with the preparations to make the wedding day perfect for the families.

The wedding took place on a crisp, cold but bright December afternoon. The private chapel looked beautiful, with banners and flaming torches hung from the walls and everywhere decorated with fir, holly and ivy. Above the altar was a huge bough of mistletoe. The families gathered in the chapel in their finery, waiting for the young bride. When she appeared in the doorway, there was an audible gasp, she looked so enchanting. She was a tall, elegant young woman, with skin as pale as milk. She wore a long-sleeved dress of green velvet. She carried a small bouquet of winter greenery and in her long red hair she wore a circlet of mistletoe, the berries standing out like pearls.

The ceremony was long and by the time the newlyweds joined their families and guests in the main hall of the castle, the night was dark and strung with stars. When they entered the hall, which was full of colour and brightness, the young bride broke her customary composure, clapping her hands in glee at the sight of the guests, the tables of food and drink, the musicians on the gallery and the large fires burning, and beaming in excitement at the thought of all the dancing, games and merrymaking ahead. As she spun round and round, much to the delight of her new husband and the guests, she suddenly stopped, clapped her hands giddily and said, 'Gifts, we must give our gifts!'

The mothers were given necklaces of fine gold and jewels, the fathers heavy cloaks of magnificent velvets. There was even a gift for the ever-helpful steward: a silver, long-bladed knife with a handle encrusted with pearls.

The celebrations went on well into the night. Everyone enjoyed the festivities, but the young bride seemed to be having the time of her life, dancing and laughing and spending time with all the guests. In fact, she seemed to be enjoying the night so much that some of the guests wondered if the couple would ever actually retire to the bridal chamber. In the end, the bride's mother took her to one side and whispered in her ear that really it was time for the revelry to end, but the young woman said loudly, 'Oh please no, I am enjoying this so much. Can we at least play one last game?'

Many of the guests looked at each other with raised eyebrows but, well, it was her wedding night and she should be able to choose how she spent it.

Gregory took the hands of his young wife and asked, 'Well, what shall it be, my love?'

Hide and seek was decided upon. Gregory stood with his face to the wall and counted to one hundred in Latin. The rest of the guests ran off to hide. When Gregory had finished counting, he turned around to begin his search.

Some of the guests were easy to find; their feet stuck out from below a tapestry they had squeezed behind, or there was uncontrollable laughter from behind a large, opened door. The guests squealed in delight as the game progressed. More and more of them were discovered and then they too joined in the search. After some time Gregory realised that everyone had now been found ... all except the bride.

The game and its intriguing search continued. She certainly seemed to have found a wonderful hiding place. But as time went on, small groups of guests began to hold back from the search, wondering if this had all been a trick on the part of the bride. If, as the rumours had suggested, she really did have a lover, had she used the pretence of a game of hide and seek to give herself a chance to escape with her lover?

The guests quietly began to withdraw and depart until at last it was only Gregory, the two sets of parents and the steward left to search. They did continue for a while but eventually, Gregory's father took him to one side and suggested what everyone else had been thinking.

'No!' shouted Gregory, 'She wouldn't do that to me, she loved me, I know she did!', and he frantically continued his search. The bride's father nodded to the steward, who immediately ran to help Gregory. The castle was robed in darkness and shadows, and no matter how frantically Gregory and the steward searched, she could not be found. In the end, the steward persuaded Gregory to wait for the light of the morning.

When the winter sun rose and shone brightly, Gregory and the steward searched the castle again but there was still no sign of her. Over the next few days, the two men searched the grounds around the castle and then began visiting the little houses and shops that surrounded the castle.

The entourage of the bride's family packed their things together and with heavy hearts began their journey home, distraught at the realisation of what their daughter had obviously planned and carried out.

Gregory and the steward, meanwhile, widened their search, concentrating on the little towns that were near the castle and the rugged countryside between them, but to no avail. Everyone by now had heard the story and were distressed and embarrassed to speak to Gregory but that was no concern to him, he KNEW she would not have left him on their wedding night, and he had to find her.

The hopeless search continued. Gregory and the faithful steward covered huge tracts of land, hardly ever returning to the castle.

The more time the two men spent together, the closer they became. The servant–master relationship slowly changed to one of true friendship, as Gregory began to rely more and more on the slightly older, protective steward. The steward took charge of the search – he arranged places to sleep, even if it was under a hedgerow, found food for them and talked to strangers. With time, it was almost as if the journey and time spent together took over from the actual search itself. The two of them became as one; they thought each other's thoughts, they ate from the same plate and shared the same bed; they became more than friends, lovers.

After many years of travelling and searching, it is said that they were found one morning following a particularly freezing cold night, frozen to death in a lonely shepherd's croft, Gregory lying in the arms of the steward, even in death protected by him.

During the search Gregory had hardly ever returned to the castle, only for the funerals of his parents, and so the buildings and the land had fallen into disrepair. As soon as official word of Gregory's death had been made public, another branch of the family moved into the castle to make it their family home, but without success, and so it was for many generations to come. It seemed as though the castle had become a cold and uninviting place.

Many years later, the castle was passed to more distant relations and a newly married couple took up residence. The young wife was determined to make this a home for her family. She decided that to begin with, all the old furniture and fittings should be removed and replaced; it should all be thrown into the courtyard and burned!

The servants began the work and soon the courtyard began to pile high with furniture, tapestries and other clutter.

Two servants had begun work on a tower at the far end of the castle. There was a single room to each floor, and they threw the junk they found down the stairs for other servants to drag to the central bonfire. At last they reached the very top floor and after having moved many things, they found a large chest. It was a sturdy piece, expertly carved with a heavy lid.

'Surely the mistress will not want to burn this fine piece?' they said, and they ran to fetch her.

The lord and lady came into the room with a group of other servants and marvelled at the beautiful box. The wife giddily clapped her hands, saying, 'It's beautiful, I wonder what's in it ... open it quickly.'

The latch was freed, and everyone gathered in closely as four servants manhandled the heavy lid. It crashed open and all had to turn away coughing and laughing at the huge cloud of dust it caused. When the dust had at last settled, they all rushed forward to look inside, but all recoiled in horror.

For lying inside were the desiccated remains of a young woman, contorted in despair, as she had obviously scrabbled to escape her coffin. Her green velvet dress was moth eaten, her dried face contorted in a captured scream and the skeletal fingers caught up in the remains of tangled, knotted red hair crowned with what seemed to be a circlet of dried leaves.

They all stood in silence at this horrific find, while a myriad of questions filled their minds ...

'Who was she?'

'How long had she been there?'

'Who had put her in there?'

'Why had she not been found before?'

And, 'Who would have secured the latch using a silver, long-bladed knife with a handle encrusted with pearls?'

ACKNOWLEDGEMENTS

Jane Metson for her meticulous first read-throughs and her constant support and encouragement.

Janet Dowling and Vonnie Denton for their invaluable support and first read-throughs.

Umi Sinha for her incredible work and being patient with me, as she carried out the first edit.

Mike O'Leary for first suggesting this project to me.

Alex James for their generous financial support in getting this collection ready for publication.

The venues that hosted my storytelling when I was experimenting with these stories, especially Leicester, Stafford and Lichfield.

Rebecca Burns for her guidance.

Daisy dog.

Joni Mitchell.

Oscar Wilde.

Katrice Horsley.

Martyn Elton for being in my life. When 'things' got fraught putting this book together, his continued support, encouragement and technical advice, kept me going.

Love you.

ABOUT THE AUTHOR

After living in Spain and France and travelling around Europe, Kevin now lives with his husband Martyn in Leicestershire.

Kevin is a painter, writer and former teacher. He has been a professional storyteller for over twenty years. As a storyteller, role player and historical interpreter, he has worked in museums and heritage sites bringing alive historic and literary incidents, characters and periods in time. Much of his work involved the research of storylines and stories for specific sites. He also performed his stories in theatres, clubs and festivals to adult audiences. His last performance piece was called *Faerie Wanting to Meet Unicorn*, a series of LGBTQ+ stories, four of which appear in this collection.

He is an experienced actor with local theatre, radio and TV credits. He has a small studio in his garden, his sanctuary, where he paints. Visit his website at www.kevinwalker-storyteller.com.

IF YOU ENJOYED THIS TITLE FROM THE HISTORY PRESS

978 0 7509 9493 4

The destination for history
www.thehistorypress.co.uk